Novelist and essayist Gianluca M[...] [born]
in 1971. His most recent titles i[nclude ...]
dalla luce and *Blackout*, his first *roman noir*. When not
writing, Gianluca Morozzi supports Bologna Football Club,
collects graphic novels and listens to The Who and Bruce
Springsteen.

BLACKOUT

Gianluca Morozzi

Translated by Howard Curtis

BITTER LEMON PRESS
LONDON

BITTER LEMON PRESS

First published in the United Kingdom in 2008 by
Bitter Lemon Press, 37 Arundel Gardens,
London W11 2LW

www.bitterlemonpress.com

First published in Italian as *Blackout* by
Ugo Guanda Editore S.p.A., Parma, 2004

Bitter Lemon Press gratefully acknowledges the financial assistance
of the Arts Council of England

A CIP record for this book is available from the
British Library

ISBN: 978–1–904738–32–9

Typeset by Alma Books, Richmond, Surrey
Printed and bound by
Cox & Wyman Ltd. Reading, Berkshire

To Giorgio and Elena

"And if you were given the possibility of doing whatever you liked, without anyone being able to judge you or punish you, without anyone saying, 'Enough! Stop it!' how far would you push yourself? How far have we gone?"

Grant Morrison, *The Invisibles*

Ferro

Ferro washes the knife under the tap, whistling *Don't Be Cruel*, and the blood drains away, a pale, washed-out red.

As far as Aldo Ferro is concerned, music began and ended with Elvis, there was nothing before Elvis, and there's been nothing since Elvis. Once Jesus has come down to earth, he always says, who's going to be satisfied with your common-or-garden prophet? This boast always makes an impression on his wife's women friends.

He comes out of the bathroom, toying with the knife. The only light in the shack is a naked bulb hanging from the ceiling. The windows are blacked out by blankets nailed into the wooden frame. Outside, beyond the trees, the dark sky is lightening to the colour of asphalt. It's almost dawn.

The young man tied to the chair hasn't yet come to. Aldo Ferro moves around him, with his snakeskin shoes, his sideburns, his shirt with the country-style embroidery, the rings of sweat under his armpits. It isn't that it's hot – you can actually breathe in this shack in the mountains, not like in town, where the muggy August heat leaves you gasping even at five in the morning. No, it was the precision work that's made him sweat. He's spent all night doing precision work.

The young man moves his head slightly and gives a feeble whimper. Aldo Ferro smiles and hums a classic, *Heartbreak*

9

Hotel, even breaking into a stiff little dance, with the knife in his hand, rather like Mr Pink before he cut off the cop's ear.

Ferro has seen the original version of *Reservoir Dogs*. Not the one with the stupid cuts they made for TV, where you saw Mr Pink – or was it Mr Orange? – dancing to *Stuck in the Middle with You* in front of the cop, then suddenly the bastards put in a shot of the ceiling. In the original version, you actually saw the cop's ear being cut off.

A first glimmer of orange light filters into the room from behind the curtains. With some difficulty, the young man opens his eyes.

Ferro's lips widen in a wicked smile. It's show time.

He positions the video camera. It's one of those professional ones that work even at low light levels. Ferro can never concentrate when the lights are too bright.

He pulls another chair over, the back of it facing the young man, and sits down. He covers his face with his son's Darth Maul mask, switches on the camera, and shines the torch in the young man's face.

"Wake up, kid, it's morning. Up you get now, your cornflakes are on the table."

The young man's name is Alex. He has a tribal tattoo on his right biceps, three piercings in his ear, a Sex Pistols T-shirt, and emerald green eyes. He is tied to the wooden chair by his wrists and ankles. He wriggles, unsettled by the light and still groggy from the sedatives.

"Come on, you'll be late for school," Aldo Ferro says, laughing. "Something tells me you haven't sussed it out yet. You're wondering where you are, what's happening, aren't you? It was the same for me, you know, when they put me under for my operation. Gallstones. Not very pleasant. I'm fine now, but when I came to, I had no idea where I was or what had happened."

He picks something up from the floor, something that looks like a soft mask, and hangs it on the back of the chair, grotesque and inanimate. "Let me help you," he continues. "Let's reconstruct your movements; that'll wake you up, I'm sure."

Alex doesn't say a word. He moves his numb head in a circle, trying to find something to hold on to in the real world.

"Listen to me, kid," Ferro continues, in a low, ingratiating voice. "Do you remember where you were last night? If you don't, I'll tell you. You were at the Pink Cadillac. That nice open-air club, the one up in the hills, with the Cadillac-shaped pool. You went there to get away from the heat, I imagine; the city's deadly this time of year. Do you remember the Pink Cadillac? Do you remember walking up to the bar and asking for a beer?"

Very slowly, Alex moves his head up and down.

Ferro smiles. "Good. So, you walked up to the bar and asked for a beer, and I was the one who served you. Every now and again I like to help out the girls behind the bar. I used to be really good at making cocktails, like Tom Cruise in that film, remember? I was just the same, I knew all the tricks, a real juggler. Anyway, I was the one who served you your beer. Having first put a particular pill in it." He gives a derisive smile, uncovering his teeth under the Darth Maul mask. "To be honest, it was a close-run thing between you and this other kid. A dead ringer for Kurt Cobain, hair in

11

front of his face, a real hangdog look, I was quite keen on him too. Do you know why I picked you in the end? Why you won out against that other loser?" He leans forward. "Because of that fucking T-shirt. Because of the Sex Pistols. Those stupid punks who pissed all over Elvis." He scratches his chin. It's hot under the mask. "I saw you finish your beer, I was watching you from a distance, waiting for the pill to start working. And when you staggered to the toilet, more dead than alive, I went to get you and put you in my car. And I brought you here." He chuckles. "So you see, my friend, if you'd left home last night wearing a Hard Rock Café T-shirt, or a Brazil World Champions T-shirt, or a Rolling Stones T-shirt, that sad Kurt Cobain lookalike would be here now. When you get down to it, it's just like if I'm walking along the street, and I stop for a moment to tie my shoelaces, and a flowerpot falls half an inch from my nose instead of on my head. Or I get to a junction just as the lights turn red and in a fraction of a second I have to decide whether I'm going to brake or accelerate, and there's no way I can know that there's a lorry coming from the other side with a drunk driver at the wheel, right? My whole future depends on what I choose in that fraction of a second. Well, you couldn't have known either, maybe that T-shirt isn't even yours and you can't stand the Sex Pistols, maybe it's your brother's but it was the only clean one you could find; tough luck, it helped me make my choice, and that's how it goes. Obviously, I'm saying all this just to give you time to regain full consciousness, because I need you awake. If a person does a good job, a bit of precision workmanship, he wants it to be appreciated. So, tell me, you're with us now, can you talk?"

"Yes," Alex mumbles.

Aldo Ferro smiles. "Good." With his thumb and index finger, he takes the soft mask from the chair back. He moves the beam of the torch away from Alex's face, and shows him the mask in the light from the naked bulb. "Do you know what this is?"

Alex is silent for a moment, then says, "No."

"Haven't you ever read Garth Ennis? *Preacher*? *Texas or Death*?"

"No."

"Really? So what kind of comics do you read? Manga, I bet. Or Dylan Dog. Take a closer look. Doesn't it remind you of anything? Don't you remember when you last saw it?"

Alex swallows. "No."

"Didn't you see it yesterday morning, for instance? When you were combing your hair, cleaning your teeth? Looking at yourself in the mirror?"

Slowly, very slowly, the realization dawns on Alex.

Gradually, his emerald-green eyes open wide, making a striking contrast with the exposed flesh.

And he looks at his own face dangling between Aldo Ferro's thumb and index finger.

"Oh, I could have been a much bigger bastard," Ferro says. "I could have left you without your eyelids, then watched you trying to close your eyes."

A strange, nagging screech emerges from Alex's throat. Like the squealing of a pig with its throat cut, or a woman's scream, sharp and interminable.

Ferro chuckles, gets to his feet and says, "Listen, I'm

13

going to take a nap, all that cutting tires you out. My in-laws are expecting me for lunch at their house by the sea, and I can't very well fall asleep on the table. I'll leave your face here, on your knees. If you're good and don't cause any trouble, I might put it back on tomorrow."

He goes upstairs and lies down on the bed.

Ignoring the sharp, interminable scream from downstairs.

Ferro sleeps for two hours, then goes back downstairs, waves goodbye to Alex, gets in his car, and sets off in the direction of the sea, humming *Can't Help Falling in Love*.

By midday he is on the terrace of the house in Cattolica, with his wife Gloria, his son Jacopo and his in-laws, slowly eating his fish and sipping at his white wine. His father-in-law is reading the newspaper and smoking a cigar, while his mother-in-law walks back and forth between the terrace and the kitchen, muttering, "You shouldn't read or smoke at table," but no one's listening.

Ferro turns to his father-in-law. "So, Franco," Ferro says, with his mouth full, "what's in the paper? Are we bombing another Middle Eastern country?"

"We're pissing on those Bedouin from a great height," his father-in-law, the General, replies, without taking his eyes off the newspaper. "Pissing on them from a great height."

"Mind your language in front of the boy," Gloria says, busy picking the bones clean of fish. Ferro looks at his son, who is eating very quickly, gulping down the fried fish almost without chewing it.

"Gloria," he says, "our son's getting fatter every day. You

14

and your mother spoil him too much, he's going to be obese."

Jacopo carries on eating as if he wasn't the one being talked about.

Gloria shrugs her shoulders and drinks a glass of white wine. When she speaks again, she changes the subject. "Do you really have to work on August Bank Holiday?" she asks, chewing. "Can't Garbarino replace you for one night?"

Aldo Ferro laughs out loud. "Darling, I wouldn't trust Garbarino with the remote control to the garage. You know what the club's like on August Bank Holiday."

Gloria snorts. Jacopo gulps down a whole glass of Coke and lets out a loud burp. Gloria cuffs him on the back of his neck, but Jacopo doesn't take any notice, just carries on eating like a drain.

Beneath the terrace, the beach is slowly emptying, as the bathers go back to their hotels for lunch. Ferro stretches, rubs his stomach, he's eaten too much, dammit. Not to mention the wine, the sea air, the sun. He's looking forward to taking a nap after lunch, lying in the sun with the sound of the waves in the background.

"We're pissing on those Bedouin from a great height," the General says again, eyes still fixed on the newspaper.

"Mind your language in front of the boy," Gloria repeats mechanically, struggling with the fish bones.

It's later, and all five of them are on the beach, enjoying the early afternoon sun. Ferro is relaxing on the sunbed, soaked in suntan oil. He's wearing a baseball cap with the word Ferrari on it, dark glasses and red trunks. Gloria is next to him, on a deckchair, half in the shade, doing a crossword. Jacopo is sitting on the sand under the beach umbrella, the melting chocolate from his Magnum Double dripping onto the pages of the Dylan Dog comic he's reading. His in-laws are a bit further away, sitting on two beach chairs. She's absorbed in a women's magazine, while the General, in a striped shirt and brown shorts, is sitting upright with his chest out and his arms folded, staring at some vague point beyond the sea and glowering every now and again at the kids playing football near the foreshore.

"So, Aldo, are you really sure about this?" Gloria asks, without looking up from her crossword.

"We've already talked about it," Aldo mutters drowsily.

"I can't understand why you want our son to feel different from everyone else. Jacopo already has a complex about being fat."

"I've told you a thousand times. You and your mother have to stop stuffing him full of food." He lowers his voice. "Your mother seems to think the only way a child can show his grandparents he loves them is to have two helpings of everything. Stop stuffing him full of food and you'll see, he'll lose weight and his complexes will disappear. As for giving him a mobile, come on now, he's only a child."

"As if other children didn't have mobiles. The hairdresser's son has one. Rita's son has one."

"Not exactly the most impressive examples."

"What's that got to do with it, Aldo? At this age, children just want to be the same as their friends. If a classmate has something and they don't, they feel inferior. It was like that with the trainers, you remember the trainers? Or that crummy bag you wanted to send poor Jacopo to school with. There are plenty of small cheap mobiles around,

16

you find them everywhere, I saw a couple of them at the shopping mall the other day, I was going to buy one without even asking you."

"Come on, Gloria, do you think this is about money? As if we didn't have enough money to buy a mobile phone. No, it's a matter of principle. I don't want the boy to grow up spoilt. If he wants a mobile, let him earn it. Let him wash my car, repaint his room, clean the house. To get something, you have to do something. If he shows willing, if he shows he can work hard, we'll buy him his mobile. What's wrong with that?"

Gloria snorts, and shakes her head. "Seems to me you're still living in your father's time. I know I'd feel a whole lot easier if Jacopo had a mobile on him when he came home from school."

Ferro laughs. "Oh sure, four stops on the bus. Anything can happen to our son in four stops."

Gloria has a brainwave. She puts down her puzzle magazine and looks at her husband wide-eyed. "I know what we'll do! I'll give Jacopo my phone, it's so old by now I'm ashamed to take it out of my handbag, and I'll buy a new one for myself. The kind that takes photos and lets you send them like texts. What do you say?"

Ferro rolls over onto his back and turns the peak of his cap round. "All these mobile phones are driving you crazy. A phone is a phone. It's for calling people, not taking photos."

"Paola has a phone that takes photos," Gloria says, glumly.

"Gloria, sweetheart. You're becoming just like your son. You want to be the same as your friends so you don't feel inferior."

Gloria shrugs irritably and falls silent. She goes back to her crossword.

A black peddler stops by Ferro's in-laws' beach umbrella and shows them some sunglasses and small bracelets, saying, "Well, friend?" a couple of times. The General's lips curl, and he stares off into the distance, pretending not to see or hear him. He keeps the same pose until the black kid shuffles away towards the next umbrella.

Ferro relaxes, with the sun beating on his back.

He thinks about how Gloria used to be, before her hips broadened. He remembers the night they met, how he offered her a cigarette on the edge of the dance floor at the Grotte, while the DJ was pumping out a dance track by the Communards, and how hypnotized he was by those incredible turquoise eyes.

The first time she got into his car, he put the Bruce Springsteen song *Gloria's Eyes* on the stereo. Ferro hated the song, but he respected Springsteen. Springsteen was a fan of Elvis. Someone who knew the distance between the master and the pupil. Someone who'd once climbed the walls of Graceland to meet the King and play him a song he'd written for him, and when the guards had stopped him his friend had cried out, "That's Bruce Springsteen! He's famous! He's been on the cover of *Time!*"

With these pleasant thoughts of Elvis and Bruce Springsteen, Ferro falls asleep.

Late in the afternoon, he goes inside the house and takes a slow unhurried shower, washing the sand and sweat out of his skin. He gets out of the shower, puts on his bathrobe, and switches on the TV. He presses the teletext button and goes to the page that has the latest news.

Young man from Bologna missing, the teletext says. *There are no clues as to his whereabouts. The police are investigating his last known movements.* Etcetera, etcetera.

Ferro gives a derisive smile and wipes his wet hair.

When the sun starts to set behind the trees, Ferro gets back in his car, waves goodbye to his wife, son and in-laws, and heads back in the direction of the city, humming *Burning Love.*

He drives up into the hills, negotiating the bends until he reaches the Pink Cadillac, which is at the top of the highest hill.

The evening hasn't got going yet. The finest open-air club in Bologna is getting ready to come to life – the commercial dance floor, the Latin-American dance floor, the main bar, the Cuban bar, the Shiatsu massage corner, the famous Cadillac-shaped swimming pool ready to be filled with foam. Ferro leaves his car in the staff car park and waves to the security guard. From the car park, when the wind brushes aside the leaves of the trees, you can see all the lights of the city shining in the darkness like little suns behind the branches.

Ferro walks through the club, saying hello to the barmaids, the DJs, the hostesses, firing them up for the evening, with a joke or a personal tip for each of them. He learned that when he was the manager and coach, as well as one of the players, of an amateur football team, and he used to go round the changing room encouraging every single one of the players, even those likely to stay on the bench.

19

The last person he says hello to is the new barmaid.

Her name's Sonja and she's from Lecce. A luscious twenty-three-year-old with dark, curly hair and that sinuous, unlikely J in the middle of her name.

Aldo Ferro has always liked women with long curly hair going down to their arses.

His partner, Garbarino, comes out of the little office behind the bar, and as he passes he smiles and whispers, "Is the bet on?"

Ferro gives him a thumbs-up sign and slips behind the bar, ready to run through the whole of his Tom Cruise repertoire, and to win the bet – which is all about Sonja from Lecce.

"How tanned you are, Signor Ferro," Sonja warbles. "Have you been to the seaside?"

"Sonja, honeybun, you know the first thing you have to remember if you don't want to get sacked from this job?" Ferro says, in a reassuring voice to make it clear he's joking. "The first thing you absolutely have to remember, if you don't want to be sacked, is to always call your boss Aldo."

Sonja smiles, revealing perfect white teeth. "How tanned you are, Aldo."

"Good girl," he says, with a mocking smile, and feels a pleasant warmth in his groin. "I like barmaids who learn fast, honeybun."

Then all of them – the barmaids, the DJs, the hostesses – take their places in the Pink Cadillac, like a team lined up in midfield waiting for the starting whistle.

And the evening gets under way.

Those citizens of Bologna who have remained in the city emerge from their lairs after a Saturday spent indoors with their fans and air conditioning turned up to maximum. Escaping from the near-deserted, furnace-like city, they come up to the hills dreaming of cool air and the Cadillac-shaped swimming pool.

Among the first to arrive are the three men Aldo Ferro calls his fan club. Three grizzled but fun-loving lawyers who hang around his clubs, because, as they always say, "Wherever Aldo is, that's where the fun is."

Ferro greets them playfully by blowing kisses. The lawyers are propping up the bar. "Aldo," one of them whispers, "fifty on the new barmaid."

Ferro looks at Sonja out of the corner of his eye. She's mixing a cocktail, and doesn't hear.

"Fifty to me if I win," he hisses, with a devilish grin, "and a hundred to you if I lose. Just to show you how confident I am."

The lawyer laughs, and shakes his hand. "Good old Ferro. Damn it, you're still the best!"

Ferro walks away, wiggling his hips, much to the amusement of the three lawyers.

He's never yet lost a bet with the fan club. There's no way he can disappoint them; they're actually happy when they lose. The bets depend on absolute trust, because there's often no way of verifying the result, but nobody would dare cheat. It's not about the money. It's a question of personal ethics.

Ferro now has two bets on. One specific one with Garbarino, and another more general one with the lawyers. Both bets, the specific and the general, are to do with Sonja, the luscious barmaid from Lecce.

It's time to get to work.

Ferro starts running through his repertoire. The fan club can barely contain their enthusiasm. He mixes cocktails to a dance rhythm, twirling glasses in the air, and with each trick he performs he casts a sidelong glance at the curly-haired Sonja to see what her reaction is.

From the bar, the music being played on the Latin-American dance floor can be heard loud and clear, and Ferro takes advantage of it to start moving in for the kill. Every time he brushes against Sonja as he rushes from one customer to another, he breaks into a little dance and puts his arm around her waist for a few moments. She laughs and makes no attempt to escape. It's a good sign.

Ferro dashes from one end of the bar to the other, greets a familiar face, then another familiar face, makes a gin and lemon, puts him arm round Sonja again, breaks into another dance, squeezes her tighter. Every now and again, he winks at his fan club, and the lawyers laugh. "Good old Ferro, he's in great form," they say, jubilant over each of his spectacular pieces of choreography.

He feels at home. He's the coach of the Pink Cadillac and one of the players.

After a particularly elaborate number, preparing five tequila bum bums while performing a magnificent pirou-ette, Ferro looks up, full of adrenalin, and sees his fan club in raptures, Sonja's admiring glances, the sea of heads swarming between the two bars, the sea of heads on the two dance floors, the sea of heads in the foam-filled swimming pool, and there's nothing that gives him a bigger kick, there's nothing to compare with the moment when *his* club vibrates in perfect harmony, like a living organism. Nothing to compare with it.

Ferro wins the bet with the fan club just before closing time, when the Pink Cadillac is already nearly empty.

He and Sonja disappear into the staff toilets. It's child's play. She's as ready and willing as an ostrich with its head in the sand.

Sonja invites him back to her place. There, Ferro scores two more goals, on the almost double bed under the Ligabue poster. The first goal scored the standard way, from the front, the second one from the rear.

It's this second goal that wins him his specific bet with Garbarino.

Afterwards, Sonja falls asleep almost immediately. Ferro lies there for a while looking at the radio-alarm, which shows the time as 4:49, the phosphorescent numbers casting a glow over the copy of *The Little Prince* on the bedside table. Then he too falls asleep.

He has a dark and disturbing dream.

He dreams he's a prisoner and he's escaping by boring a hole in the wall, a hole which leads from the cell to a natural tunnel through a mountain, a tunnel so narrow that a man can barely crawl along it.

Ferro escapes from the cell by crawling backwards, on his back. Using his feet and elbows to propel himself along.

He doesn't know why he has to move in that uncomfortable position. He knows that the tunnel is too narrow for him to be able to turn, and so he just keeps moving, heels, elbows, heels, elbows, his head outstretched in the darkness. He crawls backwards for miles and miles.

He has a panic attack and clutches at the rock, in the world of dreams. In the real world, he clutches at the pillow.

He has just realized that he has a mountain, an entire mountain, above him. The weight of an entire mountain bearing down on his poor flesh and fragile bones. He lies still for a long time, his nose and mouth a fraction of an inch from the cold rock.

Then he hears a noise coming from the direction of the cell, the direction of his feet. Something crawling along the tunnel.

Something like a huge, repulsive worm, coming slowly, unhurriedly towards him.

So he starts moving more quickly, ever more quickly, until his elbows, back and hands are grazed, and his shoes are scraped at the heels. Then he sees a light. Crazy with joy, he continues crawling backwards, as the light gets stronger and stronger.

At last, his head and shoulders are out of the tunnel. He breathes in the clean air, and looks up at the sky. Then he looks down, in so far as it's possible with almost his whole body still in the tunnel.

The tunnel has opened out in the middle of a smooth cliff wall. With a sheer drop to a stormy sea.

The sea rages, hundreds of feet below his head. Absurdly, his head is bang in the middle of a mountainside.

And that repulsive disgusting worm is still slithering along, very close to his feet now.

He wakes up with his heart in his mouth, bathed in sweat and shaking all over. He has to make an effort to emerge from the nightmare of the worm and the tunnel back into the reality of the pillow, Sonja asleep, the radio-alarm showing the time as 4:58.

He gets up without waking Sonja and takes a shower.

He stands under the jet of water for a long time. Drawing concentric circles with his finger in the steam on the shower wall.

He was expecting the police to show up at the Pink Cadillac at some point last night. Not that he was afraid. But he was expecting it.

Of course, Alex had been alone at the club, without his friends. Maybe all his friends were away and he'd been the only one to spend all day in the scorching city, or maybe he'd come up to the hills without telling anyone.

In any case, even if the police had come, it wouldn't have caused Ferro any sweat. He could simply have said, yes, I think I saw a young guy in a Sex Pistols T-shirt, I remember him because of the T-shirt, I served him a beer, then I lost him in the crowd, I was behind the bar till closing time. The perfect alibi.

No one had seen Ferro go into the toilets a few minutes after Alex. The toilets were a bit isolated from the rest of the club, behind the tall trees, and it had been a dark, moonless night.

No one had seen him come out of the toilets with the unconscious Alex, he's absolutely sure of that. If he'd run into anyone, he'd had an excuse ready. "He's had a bit too much to drink," he would have said. "I'm taking him for a bit of air to sober him up." But he hadn't met anyone.

He had gone round the back and through the fence

between the trees, in order to avoid the security guard. Emerging from the shadows, he had quickly opened the boot of the car, which he had left in the furthest, darkest part of the car park. He had locked Alex in the boot, keeping his eyes open for any movement from the security guard. Then he had again slipped into the shadows and under the fence, and almost immediately reappeared behind the bar, his usual merry self. Ready to do his Tom Cruise tricks until closing time. When he would get back in the car and drive to the shack, with Alex asleep in the boot.

Ferro comes out of the shower and dresses in silence, without waking Sonja.

He leaves the building. The night air is still warm.

He drives calmly to the shack in the mountains. He leaves the car just off the path, switches off the engine and the lights, but doesn't get out straight away. First, he opens the jewel case where he keeps his cocaine, and does another line. Then he puts on the black-and-red Darth Maul mask, walks to the shack and goes in.

Alex has stopped screaming. He's breathing very heavily now, and trembling all over like a horse. He has vomited on his own face, his jeans, his shoes.

"Look what you've done," Ferro says, searching for a pair of gloves. "What a mess." With two fingers, he takes the face from Alex's knees and washes it under the tap. Then he switches on the video camera, and sits down facing Alex.

He stares at him in silence for a few minutes, stares straight at his green, vacuous eyes in the midst of the exposed flesh. Then he says, "You know, I really don't like you at all with your skin all flayed like that."

He turns the mask over in his hands, the soft mask that was Alex's face.

"Let me explain. Since I've been alone, I've had to improvise. The Dentist used to make all the decisions, I just listened and copied him. He was the one who had all the creative ideas, he'd studied a lot." He breaks off to adjust the Darth Maul mask, then resumes. "He'd read all these medieval books, you know, about torture during the Inquisition. They could do things you wouldn't believe, techniques handed down from ancient Atlantis, according to the Dentist. A very cultured man, the Dentist." He stands up, opens a drawer and takes out a plastic bag. He comes back and sits down again with the plastic bag in one hand and Alex's face in the other.

"Those people could keep a man alive even after they took out his internal organs. Can you imagine? They could keep him conscious after reducing him to an almost empty shell, just a trunk and a skull." Slowly, unhurriedly, he opens the plastic bag. "The Dentist knew all the methods they used during the Inquisition. He could send a man to hell while he was still alive. We had a bet once, about the window cleaner. He said he could keep him alive for more than ten days, and I said ten days was impossible, he'd never keep him alive as long as that. Well, do you know how long he kept him alive for? *Fourteen* days. Fourteen. And if I hadn't overdone it, if I hadn't got carried away, we could have kept him in this world even longer. Even though there was less than half of that nigger left, I swear."

27

He pauses for a long time. Alex stares at him with eyes like those of a cow chewing the cud, but doesn't make a sound.

"Anyway," Aldo Ferro continues, "the Dentist isn't here any more. The shack belongs to me now and I have to improvise. I pick up ideas from all kinds of places, films, comics, whatever. And I've decided that, with your face sliced off like that, you look really disgusting."

He toys a little more with the soft mask.

"That's why," he says, articulating his words very clearly, and holding back a sneer, "I've decided to put your face back on."

He opens the plastic bag.

He takes out the hammer.

And the box of nails.

What was it the Dentist used to say? Ferro thinks when his work is done, lying on the bed, staring up at the ceiling. *What was that expression he always used?*

"A pound of flesh . . ." he used to say. "A pound of flesh, we deserve our pound of flesh. We work like mules," he used to say, "and after working like mules, we deserve our pound of flesh." Then he'd put on something from his video collection, one of those snuff movies.

Both Ferro and the Dentist enjoyed those movies for a while. Then they both got bored with them.

"It's all so unimaginative," the Dentist had snorted, watching yet another eye-catching but derivative torture. "They have no idea how to stimulate the viewer. I could do better than that."

* * *

And so they started making videos themselves.

Right here, in the shack. They had the two freezers under the trapdoor, they had the cameras. And they had all the Dentist's concoctions.

And now I'm alone, Ferro thought, looking up at the ceiling.

That idiot, that stupid idiot. The Dentist and his daughter get a consignment of pills they've never heard of and never tested, and the two idiots knock them back as if they were aspirin.

He was especially sorry about the Dentist's daughter. He always liked the Dentist's daughter, the arse she had on her, you could really go to work on an arse like that.

One time when it was raining hard and he was in his car, he had seen the Dentist's daughter standing at the bus stop outside the gym.

He had given her a lift, and after a while had tried to kiss her. He had insisted and insisted, but she wouldn't let him touch her; all she'd agreed to was to give him a slow handjob, making sure she didn't get herself dirty.

Frigid bitch, Ferro had thought as he was coming.

The Dentist had accumulated enough magic potions for at least two years of videos.

Some of them they kept in the shack, some in Ferro's old bachelor apartment. Obviously, his wife didn't know he had an apartment stacked full of magic potions and videos. Every now and again Ferro would go there, pick up some magic potions, leave a new video, and disappear.

29

The apartment is on the twentieth floor of a tower block, outside Borgo Panigale.

It's already mid-afternoon by the time Ferro goes back downstairs. He admires his handiwork, Alex's green eyes, pale and vacuous behind what had been his mouth. The face nailed on upside down, and stretched tightly at the four corners.

For it to be perfect, Alex ought to whimper something like "Kill me, for God's sake kill me." Instead, he says nothing. Even his breathing is muted, a dull drone from the back of his throat.

Ferro goes into the kitchen and pours himself a glass of water from the tap. He goes back to Alex and slowly sips the water, lifting the Darth Maul mask only a little. Then he starts speaking, in a low voice.

"I have to leave you until tonight, my dear. I have to go to the Dentist's apartment, because the next step in my programme is the cutting off of the scrotum." He goes closer to Alex. "The only problem, my dear, is that when the scrotum is cut off, a lot of blood comes out. The Dentist was good at handling that kind of thing, haemorrhages were his daily bread. Between you and me, I'm not as well equipped as he was. So I need a little help from science, sweetheart, I'm going to get some more magic potions, I wouldn't want you to die on me after all the work I did with the scissors and the knife." He prepares to leave. "Say goodbye to your crown jewels, kid, these are the last hours you'll be spending together."

As he goes out, Ferro regrets coming out with such a vulgar sentence. He has ruined the whole of his speech after taking so much care over the accent, the rhythm, the cadence. Fuck, the Dentist was such a good speaker. He'll have to erase a few seconds of the soundtrack from the video.

He does another line of coke from the jewel box, then sets off towards the city.

Ferro is tempted, very tempted.

It's a risk, of course, a big risk. But it doesn't really depart from the plan.

In the original plan, after the cutting of the scrotum, there's no future for Alex. They've already had a lot of fun together, the video has gone well, that's where they should stop. Ferro hasn't yet thought of the most exciting way to kill him, but everything in its own time.

But now, in his coke- and adrenalin-fuelled mind, a crazy idea is taking shape. The most exciting way to kill him is to let him live.

Get rid of any telltale signs, and send the police to the shack in the mountains. Like that terrific scene in *Preacher*, where the police find the man tied to the chair whimpering, "Kill me" and the cop says, "I don't know if the doctors can do anything for this poor guy, he'd be better off dead."

It's a really exciting idea. Send him back into the world as he is, a dismantled and reassembled parody of a human being. Forced to live like the grotesque puppet he's become.

Could Alex identify me? Ferro wonders. *Could he give me away? I was wearing the mask, of course, but I did mention the Pink Cadillac, I told him it's my club, so it's a risk, but it's a beautiful risk, a fun risk . . . Does he still have a mind left, after*

31

what I've done to him? Enough to get me in trouble with the police?

He puts off the decision, and hums *Suspicious Minds.*

He always thinks better if he hums Elvis while he's driving.

During the August Bank Holiday, Bologna is like a stone quarry with the sun beating down on it. No one on the ring road, no one on the avenue leading to the hypermarket, nothing, no one. A desert.

I could stop the car in the middle of a roundabout, Ferro thinks, *relieve myself under a flyover, cook a meal over a camp stove, and no one would see me. Only there's this fucking damp heat which is fine for mosquitoes, yes, for fucking mosquitoes, not for people.*

He turns right towards Casteldebole, going through a red light, because there's no sign of a car on the road. He drives to the very edge of the city, where two identical twenty-storey blocks tower over the green fields. He parks beneath the towers, behind a blue Transit van which is half on the pavement and half in the road.

His bachelor apartment is on the top floor of that concrete monster.

Ferro gets out and wipes the sweat from his forehead with a handkerchief. Searching in his pocket for the keys to the apartment, he touches something hard.

The jack knife. I left the jack knife in my pocket. I've been working too hard, I'm getting absent-minded.

He opens the main door and starts across the entrance hall, heading for the two elevators.

Two people are standing in front of the elevator on the

left-hand side, a sixteen-year-old boy with a piercing in his eyebrow and a Bruce Springsteen T-shirt, and a girl with green hair wearing a uniform from a bar in the centre of town. They're both waiting. On the door of the elevator on the right is a sign saying OUT OF ORDER.

Ferro snorts in annoyance. He mutters an irritable, perfunctory "Hello" to the boy and the girl. He's never understood why you're expected to say hello to people you've never seen and don't know from Adam just because you bump into them in the same entrance hall, but that's the way it is, you have to obey a few rules in order to live with people.

The idea of sharing an elevator with strangers doesn't appeal to him at all. He's about to give up and use the stairs, but then he thinks, *Fuck, that's twenty floors on foot, in this heat.* So he resigns himself to a few seconds of forced intimacy.

At least the girl with green hair is fairly pretty.

The elevator doors open. The girl walks in first. Then the boy with the piercing. Then Ferro.

The elevator doors close.

The elevator starts to ascend.

Claudia

Claudia leaves the bar in the centre of town, her eyes watery, her lower lip quivering with anger. She walks quickly, trying to get away as fast as she can from the Pig and the air conditioning in his lousy bar and the cocktails with the little umbrellas and the chocolates they serve with the coffee.

The last thing she wants to do is cry; she wouldn't waste a tear on that grotesque, insignificant little creature. She fights back the tears, clenches her fists and walks even faster. She cried when her beloved grandmother died, and when her puppy was run over by a car – but she wouldn't waste her tears on the Pig, they'd only be tears of frustration.

The Pig's voice echoes in her head as she hurries along the ghostly back streets. "So now you're coming to work in your uniform, are you, darling? Why's that? Do you sleep in it too?"

As she was only just coming on duty, she stifled her reply.

I wouldn't come here in uniform, you filthy pig, I wouldn't spend half an hour on the bus in this lap dancer's costume, you pathetic excuse for a human being, I wouldn't come in uniform if you didn't spy on me when I change in the back room, like the piece of slime that you are.

Claudia wishes she were already at home, she wishes she could take off this uniform that makes her look like a hostess in a porn movie and get in the shower and wash away all the disgust she feels and then huddle up against Bea in her bathrobe and tell her everything and find comfort in the warmth of her arms.

But Bea's on another continent, and won't be back for two more weeks. And to get home, dammit, she has to get to the bus stop in this infernal heat and wait for a bus that'll take forever coming because it's not only Sunday but August Bank Holiday too and even when the bus comes the journey will take half an hour.

Claudia crosses the deserted Piazza Maggiore, which is like an oven. Nothing's moving anywhere in the whole of the square – a pigeon flying, a pensioner on a bicycle – nothing. August Bank Holiday Sunday, Claudia thinks, is like the winter sea in that old song, a concept the mind can't even begin to imagine.

Somewhere, an hour away on the motorway, everyone from the city has crowded onto the beaches. Looking at the Piazza Maggiore and the god Neptune rising proudly in the middle of this emptiness, Claudia remembers the cover of the first comic book she stole from her brother's collection, the one with Superman in the middle of an empty street, a newspaper whirling between the buildings, the sun setting behind his cloak, and Superman crying out in despair, "All the men, women and children in the world have disappeared. Lord, I beg you, help me, I don't want to be the last man on Earth!"

She stops to drink from the little fountain beneath the figure of Neptune, feeling the cold water run down her parched throat. She wipes her mouth with the back of her hand and looks down the acute perspective of the Via

Indipendenza, the arcades that seem to stretch endlessly towards the vanishing point. A city without people and without sound, she thinks, is like a deserted disco where the DJ keeps playing discs that no one dances to. And the usual red and orange of Bologna have turned a blinding white and yellow, on this stifling August Bank Holiday Sunday.

Then a shrill noise breaks the silence.

Claudia jumps, startled. The noise is the metallic sound of a rusty wheel. A man emerges from the shade of the Palazzo Re Enzo, a man with a long ginger beard, stooped over, one eye half-closed. He's wearing combat fatigues, has a toy two-way radio pressed to his ear, and is pushing a shopping trolley full of bags.

Claudia tenses and quickens her pace.

Moving in slow motion, the man in fatigues pushes the trolley towards the centre of the square. He spots Claudia with his good eye and yells, "Lick the ground, bitch! Lick the ground, bitch!" in a strangulated little voice. Claudia hurries out of the square and down the Via Rizzoli. The man keeps yelling, "Lick the ground, bitch!"

Claudia looks around her frantically. If the madman abandons the trolley and starts to follow her, there won't be anywhere she could hide. There's nothing open in the Via Rizzoli: a closed bar next to a closed shoe shop, a closed bookshop next to a closed optician's, a closed record shop, a closed fast-food restaurant. If the madman catches up with her and grabs her arm and breathes his foul alcohol breath in her face and yells, "Lick the ground, bitch! Lick the ground, bitch!" Claudia could scream as loud as she liked and no one would hear her. So she tenses her muscles, trying to recall her two years of judo, the orange belt. She can defend herself, if she has to.

But the madman isn't following her. He's laboriously pushing his trolley around the fountain of Neptune, shouting to himself. Claudia watches him out of the corner of her eye until she gets to the bus stop. If the madman leaves the square, she's ready to run like the wind through the side streets.

She shelters from the sun in the narrow strip of shade provided by a building, but even in the shade the heat is killing, and the bus is going to take forever, on a Sunday in summer, during August Bank Holiday.

There's no one around, no one at all. The people who live here are by the sea, the people who just work or study here are indoors, the drug dealers have all gone to the coast to do their dealing. The Pig's bar is still open, but it's the only one. The Pig would stay open even on the night of the twenty-fifth to twenty-sixth of December – all night long if he could.

She has a clear memory of the first time she met the Pig. A summer job, that had been her idea, three months in a bar in the centre of town, just until the start of the academic year. She showed up for the interview in jeans and a white T-shirt, carrying her Peruvian shoulder bag. The Pig looked at her from behind the bar with his piggy little eyes, all fat and sweaty, and said, "You're a little short."

Short? she thought. *What's he on about? I'm here to serve customers, not play basketball.*

Then the Pig eyed her up and down, judging each part of her. Her green hair, sticking up like Bart Simpson's hair.

Her big eyes like a character in a Japanese cartoon. Her small breasts. He turned his nose up.

Then his eyes came to rest on her legs. He liked her legs.

He made her put on the uniform. He had one in her size. He must have had dozens of these very low-cut, very short uniforms in the back room. For every imaginable size and shape of aspiring barmaid.

Then, while Claudia was looking at herself incredulously in the back room, squeezed into that slip of a costume like a porn movie nurse, the Pig called to her from the other side of the door, "Signorina, could I have a coffee, please?"

She went back in. The Pig was sitting at a table, pretending to be a customer.

At that moment, Claudia felt like laughing. It was like one of Bea's auditions: I'd like you to play a barmaid, signorina, bring me a coffee, let me see how you bring a coffee.

All right, she thought, *let's audition.* She made the coffee, filled a glass with water, put the cup, a chocolate, the glass and a sachet of sugar on the tray, came out from behind the bar and carried the tray to the table where the pretend customer sat.

"Slower," the Pig said. "Walk slower." She was puzzled, but slowed down.

"Wiggle your hips a bit," the Pig said. "The customers like that kind of thing."

There was no way she was going to wiggle her hips. Walking more slowly was one thing, but if the customers wanted her to do a bit of lap dancing they could at least slip some money into her cleavage, right? Frowning, she put the coffee down on the table.

The Pig watched her as she walked back to the bar, staring at her legs as revealed by the skimpy uniform. "You take too much for granted, signorina," he mumbled.

"I'm sorry?" she replied.

"You take too much for granted," the Pig repeated. "For example, who said I want a glass of still water and not sparkling water? Shouldn't you have asked me first?"

Claudia looked at him as if he were some kind of worm. She swallowed, stifled an insult, and put on a very fake smile. "I'm sorry, signore, how do you like your water, still or sparkling?"

At last, the bus arrives.

Claudia gets on quickly, making sure the madman with the shopping trolley is still walking round and round the Neptune fountain. She goes to the back of the bus and sits down. She relaxes at last.

She digs a packet of chocolate biscuits out of the Peruvian bag and eats one. As the bus turns into the Via Ugo Bassi, which looks like a post-nuclear nightmare, she puts the packet back in the bag.

She thinks about the Pig, about the first time he gave her a slap on the backside. To get her to serve the customers more quickly, he said, making a joke of it.

Or the first time she caught him spying on her as she changed in the back room.

If only she didn't need to work, dammit, if only she didn't need the money. Again she fights back the tears of anger, and looks out of the window with her arms folded and her legs stretched under the seat in front of her.

She thinks about Bea, about how much she misses Bea.

"We're in a place on the edge of the desert," Bea said the last time she gave Claudia a quick call. "It's called Erfoud. We're moving around among the dunes. I'll bring you back some sand."

Sometimes, when her longing for Bea was particularly unbearable, Claudia caught herself feeling resentment towards her. For being so far away for so long. Leaving her alone in this no man's land.

She'd immediately regret feeling that way. There was no way Bea could have let an opportunity like that go by, after struggling for so long. An international co-production, three months' filming in Morocco, with three camel trainers, falconers, the top stuntmen – it was an incredible step up, after all those shoestring budgets, all those films shot in the streets and in student bars. Bea could never say no.

But three months, dammit, is a long time. Two more weeks without Bea, two more weeks. Claudia has been keeping a little calendar, the way prisoners do, a line of Xs that keeps getting longer but still isn't long enough.

And besides, she's always been wildly jealous. God knows who Bea might meet on the set of an international co-production, what interesting people, down there in the desert, among the sand dunes.

Enough of that, Claudia thinks. She must concentrate on something, anything as long as it isn't Bea. She starts going through her precious Superman collection in her head.

She sets herself some targets, rare issues she needs to add to the collection. *The Pig's wages can't all go on tuition fees,* she thinks.

The first targets are easy ones. She doesn't want to feel too stressed when the academic year starts.

Issue 205 of the Falco series, the beginnings of Supergirl, renamed Nembo Star for the Italian market to be consistent with Superman, who was called Nembo Kid. That's an easy one to get. No problem.

Then Issue 31 of the Nembo Kid Supercomics, with the beginnings of the second Flash. That's feasible too.

Then she could hunt for No. 33 of the Falco series. The first one with Batman driving his Batmobile.

Claudia mentally updates her collection as the bus drives through Porta San Felice, leaving the walls of the city behind. Anything, just so as not to think about Bea.

Claudia never reads Italian comics, but she's always liked the story of the unfinished galleon in Dylan Dog.

Focusing on a task that's almost impossible to see through to the end, pursuing a dream that keeps getting closer but never quite arrives. That's something Claudia learned from her beloved grandma, who started to study English at the age of eighty-six.

"I know perfectly well I'll never learn English," her beloved grandma said. "But until my last day, I'll have something to aim for."

Claudia fell in love with Superman as soon as she read that comic of her brother's, the one about the last man on Earth. And she started to collect everything, every single Superman story that appeared in Italy from 1939 onwards.

If she ever completes her collection, if she finds Issue 19 of the Audacia series, where Superman is called Ciclone the Man of Steel, and Audace Issue 299 with Ciclone the

42

Man Marvel, then she'll start collecting the American comics. All the stories that have never been published in Italy.

While she's absorbed mentally in her Superman collection, a man gets on in the Via Saffi, a short, stocky man, wiping the sweat from his forehead with a handkerchief. He's breathing heavily as he gets on, as if he's suffocating. Angrily, he grabs hold of one of the windows and pulls it down, muttering, "All the windows are closed, how can you keep the windows closed, people could die in here, how can you keep the windows closed, do you want to die?"

"The air conditioning is on," Claudia says.

The man whirls round. "What did you say, signorina?" he snaps.

"The bus is air conditioned," Claudia goes on. "If you open the window, the air conditioning stops working."

The man looks as if he'd like to smash the windows with his skull, all of them, one by one. "Signorina," he gurgles from the back of his throat, "you think you can teach me how to live my life, is that it, you think you can teach me how to live my life, in order not to feel hot we need to keep the windows closed, well, that makes sense, doesn't it, I don't know what people are thinking of these days, I really don't." And he looks at her threateningly, in case she's planning to say anything more about the air conditioning and keeping the windows closed.

Claudia decides she's had enough madmen for today, after the man with the trolley. She shrugs and looks out at the Ospedale Maggiore, while the man goes and sits down near the driver, cursing the heat and the humidity and girls who think they can teach him how to live his life.

Two stops later, he gets off.

Claudia doesn't even have the strength to get up and close the window.

The bus enters a maze of iron bridges, vast roundabouts and wide streets: the north-eastern outskirts of Bologna. It passes the four identical attention-grabbing towers rising on the left, four white cubes with square windows – the biscuit tins, Bea calls them. "Anyone born in a building like that is bound to turn into a drug dealer or a pornographer," Bea says. "OK, so sometimes a genius is born in squalor, but this is beyond squalor, any kind of creative impulse soon gets snuffed out, what a nightmare, like being trapped in a shoebox." Claudia smiles as she looks at those four concrete cubes; even those concrete cubes remind her of Bea. One way or another, everything reminds her of Bea.

The bus crosses the bridge over the River Reno and turns left just after the McDonald's drive-in which is part of a service station. "It's incredible," Bea says. "When it's foggy you can't see San Luca, but from your window that huge yellow M is clearly visible. The multinationals have their own lighthouse in the fog."

Claudia shakes her head and chuckles to herself. "Even a McDonald's reminds me of Bea. I miss her to bits."

The bus moves down narrow streets named after former presidents of the Republic, turns the corner of a small shopping centre, which is closed, then turns again within view of a building site. This is an area where the city is spreading out into the countryside like an ink stain. The

44

bus swerves slightly to avoid a blue Transit van with two wheels on the pavement and two in the road and comes to a halt at the last stop, just outside where Claudia lives.

Home at last, she thinks. She's tired, irritable and hot. Instinctively, she almost says goodbye to the driver. Of the four people she's seen in the last few hours – the other three being the Pig, the madman with the shopping trolley and the man who was worried about the windows – he's been the only one not to treat her badly.

Home, for Claudia, is a white monster, twenty storeys high, its lines curiously rounded, facing an identical white monster on the other side of the small shopping centre. The twin towers, people in the area used to call them. Since those planes flew into the other twin towers they've stopped doing that; no point in attracting bad luck needlessly, and anyway, it doesn't seem quite right.

She searches for her keys in the Peruvian bag, but there's no need. A young man of about sixteen has gone in just before her, closing the main door behind him, but when he sees her coming, he turns back and opens the door to let her in, even holds it open for her, like a real gentleman. She thanks him with a smile. She's now met five people today: one was neutral, this one is kind, at least the percentage is improving.

Claudia and the boy in the Bruce Springsteen T-shirt have met a few times in the entrance hall of the building. She's always greeted him with a whispered Hi, and he always used to reply with a strained Hello, which made her feel old.

Then, a few days after she dyed her hair green, Claudia met him again on the stairs. She whispered her usual

45

Hi, and he responded with a similar Hi. Maybe her Bart Simpson hair made her look more like a young girl. Not that she felt old, at twenty-four. But having a sixteen-year-old say Hi to her instead of Hello made her feel good.

Claudia and the boy stop in front of the one elevator that's working. The one on the right has a conspicuous OUT OF ORDER sign on it. *Until a few days ago they were doing maintenance work on the left-hand one, now they've swapped over,* Claudia thinks. *Maybe after the holiday they'll have them both working. Great.*

The boy pushes the button, and they both wait in silence.

Claudia doesn't like being in elevators with strangers, but the idea of walking up nineteen floors in this unbearable early August heat, God, it makes you breathless just thinking of it. All things considered, a few seconds of forced intimacy has never killed anyone.

Then the main door opens again behind them, and a man comes in, one of the many inhabitants of this monstrosity on the edge of the city whom she's never seen.

Claudia has to stop herself smiling. The newcomer looks like Elvis Presley. Huge sideburns covering half his face, snakeskin boots, a shirt with country-style embroidery, two huge patches of sweat under his armpits. *A statistical anomaly,* she thinks. *Bologna's empty, totally empty, and in the entrance hall of this building on the edge of the known world, three people are all waiting for an elevator at the same time.*

The Elvis lookalike mumbles a curt "Hello". He and Claudia and the boy with the pierced eyebrow wait for the elevator to descend.

When the metal doors open, the boy lets Claudia walk in first.

The boy gets in second. The Elvis lookalike last.

The doors close. The elevator starts to ascend.

Tomas

Tomas is zooming along on his legendary bright-orange Vespa. He has left the city walls behind and is now lurching and clattering past the roundabouts and along the wide streets on the outskirts of town, beneath the cube-shaped towers, and across the bridge over the River Reno. He's on his way home.

My life's about to change, he thinks. The way it's about to change is so incredible that Tomas has to make an effort to keep calm, because his heart is pumping like a hammer under his Bruce Springsteen T-shirt.

In his pocket, he has a train ticket for Amsterdam.

He paid for it by selling some old discs and comics, and by ferreting in the back of his parents' drawers. Especially by ferreting in the backs of drawers.

It's incredible, Tomas thinks, passing a bus which is trundling along half-full. *Today I'm in a deserted quarry which looks like Bologna, tomorrow morning I'll be with Francesca by the canals of Amsterdam, a predictable destination, I admit, but the destination doesn't matter, as long as it's a long way from here and I'm with Francesca, that's all that matters.* At the thought of holding hands with Francesca by the canals of Amsterdam, his eyes get blurry, a big smile automatically forms on his face, a pleasant drowsiness settles at the back of his neck and under his tongue and behind his eyes, and in his mind she's all rosy cheeks and Catholic nerves, while he's a song called *Thunder Road.*

In the past few months, whenever anyone has asked him who his favourite singer is, he hasn't answered Ligabue, but Bruce Springsteen. Even though he only has one Bruce Springsteen album. And from that album he only ever listens to two songs out of the eight, always the same two, the ones that make him think of Francesca and Amsterdam and the train ticket he has in his pocket.

It was his big cousin who introduced him to that album and those two songs.

His big cousin who lives surrounded by a neatly arranged collection of CDs and LPs, and always responds to Tomas's teenage enthusiasms with a superior little smile, a bored expression, and a reference to some past giant of rock.

"The Placebos smashed their guitars on stage!" Tomas would enthuse, and the cousin would say, with his superior little smile and his bored expression, "The Who did that forty years ago."

Tomas wouldn't give up that easily. "Marilyn Manson has announced he'll kill himself on stage!" To which his cousin would reply, "David Bowie did that, when he was Ziggy Stardust."

And then Tomas played him an old song by Ligabue, one of his favourites, and the words of the song are about a boy and a girl who escape from the place where they were born so as not to become like their parents and friends, and she asks, "Where are we going?" and he replies, "We don't know, but we do know what we didn't have here." Tomas really loved that song.

His cousin listened to it and remarked, "Not bad, nice words, but now listen to the guy they got the idea from."

And he took that old Bruce Springsteen LP from the shelf and put it on the turntable and threw him the sleeve with the words of *Thunder Road* and *Born to Run.*

The effect on Tomas was instant and overpowering.

The last words of *Thunder Road,* those historic last words, were one of the first quotations he wrote at the end of an e-mail to Francesca.

Francesca was now so much part of him, as close and natural as breathing, that it was incredible to think about a time when he didn't know her. Or about the shorter length of time when they were merely two anonymous screen names.

It was at the beginning of winter that Tomas started paying frequent visits to an unofficial Pearl Jam site. Not one of the better ones, in fact, an over-emotional, poorly designed site, full of girls in love with Eddie Vedder who would debate the way he looked with a beard, without a beard, or with a Mohican, and full, too, of underage metalheads who missed the toughness of the groups' Nineties discs and accused them of going soft and flabby. Tomas would have fun stirring things up, posting opinionated messages under the screen name Leatherman, sparking debate, attracting abuse from the girls in love with Eddie Vedder and the underage metalheads, quarrelling with everyone for the silliest reasons. Whenever the discussion languished, he would invent other screen names and attack Leatherman, so that he would sometimes be carrying on an argument with himself. He really enjoyed himself creating havoc on that over-emotional, poorly de-signed site full of girls in love and underage metalheads.

Then, among all the other posts, he read one by Bee Girl. The one entitled *I hardly believe, finally the shades are raised.*

It caught his eye like a bloodstain on a black-and-white photo, that beautiful reference to the words of *Rearviewmirror*, all about leaving your nightmares behind you, seeing the monsters disappear in the rear-view mirror and almost not believing you're free and don't have to be afraid any more.

"Shit," Tomas said out loud, sitting there at his computer.

He immediately wrote a reply to that message, a very calm, admiring reply, though he couldn't avoid a slight touch of sarcasm. He was about to send it to the site, to be read by everyone, the girls in love and the underage metalheads, when he hesitated. He clicked on the little envelope under Bee Girl's name, and sent her the reply privately.

Then he waited.

He had to wait until evening for Bee Girl's reply. *I was hoping you'd respond. The famous Leatherman deigns to descend among us ordinary mortals, how come you're not playing the smart Alec this time, young man?*

Tomas drummed on the table next to the keyboard.

The Bee Girl wants war, he thought. Regretting the excessive seriousness of his first message, he replied now with one of his usual tongue-lashings.

For a week, Leatherman and Bee Girl sparred via e-mail. What happened next was like a Meg Ryan comedy.

By the second week, they couldn't do without each

other. At the beginning of the third week, they revealed themselves to each other as Tomas from Bologna and Francesca from Parma. By now they were totally dependent on each other's messages.

Tomas found himself waiting anxiously for Francesca's messages, with an intensity that made him feel sick. The best moment of the day was when he opened his e-mail and there was a message from the girl from Parma. The worst was when he opened his e-mail and there was nothing.

They decided not to send each other photos, even though they couldn't wait to see each other in real life. Photos are so flat, they both said, no photos, nothing. A couple of times Tomas was on the point of suggesting they meet in Parma. Just meet, nothing else. He didn't do it.

Meeting too abruptly might scare her. Create a distance, make her nervous. And he didn't want to scare her, create a distance, or make her nervous. He really didn't want that.

They needed an excuse, something that seemed casual and innocent. And then the seemingly casual, innocent excuse presented itself.

Red Mosquito, a Pearl Jam cover band highly thought of on that poorly designed, over-emotional website, were playing in a pub in Parma.

This was it, the seemingly casual, innocent excuse.

Are you coming here to see Red Mosquito? Francesca asked, and he replied, *Yes, I'm coming, that way I'll see what you look like.* And then, pausing for a moment before typing in the next few words, *How will I recognize you, do you have a Pearl Jam T-shirt?*

They'll all be wearing Pearl Jam T-shirts, stupid, she replied, with a smiley face next to the *stupid* to make it clear it was meant affectionately. *I'll put on a T-shirt from my favourite film, The Matrix,* she concluded, *that way I'll see what you look like too.*

Tomas travelled to Parma by train, more excited than he'd ever been in his life.

When he entered the pub, he recognized her immediately.

Without ever having seen her.

There couldn't be any doubt.

It was as if there was no one else there, in that pub full of Pearl Jam fans gathered beneath the stage where Red Mosquito were playing.

She was behind the bar, the *Matrix* T-shirt half-covered, but Tomas didn't need any T-shirt to identify her. He went up to her and said, his voice shaking slightly, "Hi, Bee Girl."

That was the moment Tomas started believing in reincarnation.

Seeing Francesca behind the bar was like spotting an old acquaintance. Like when he had seen Lisa Limone, his sweetheart from elementary school, sitting on a banquette at a Sunday afternoon disco, and he had gone up to her, pleased to see that she had become even prettier in the five years since leaving school, and had said, quite naturally, "Hi, where have you been all this time?"

Just as naturally as he now said "Hi, Bee Girl", to a girl he'd never seen before in his life.

In this life, anyway.

Francesca had a slightly asymmetrical face, and was a tiny bit cross-eyed, which Tomas found irresistible. He hated perfection. Perfection was boring.

Ignoring Red Mosquito, they talked non-stop. In the end they left, tired of shouting louder than the singer in the band, and sat down on a bench, forgetting all about the cold, and exchanged confidences about their respective families, with the steam condensing as they spoke. Like people who've known each other for years, not just for a few minutes.

Many years before, Francesca's father had been a famous comedian, the regular host of *Fast Food*, a TV show that absolutely everyone watched in the mid-Eighties.

He'd been a moderate success at first, with characters like the narcoleptic lorry driver and the kleptomaniac traffic policeman, but he hadn't really taken off until halfway through the first series of *Fast Food* – when he had appeared in orange and purple tights with his pants worn over them, and introduced himself as the defender of the weak, the protector of little old ladies, the one and only Giampi Supermaxihero. A bungling superhero, spoofing an Eighties TV movie. With his supermaxidog, supermaximobile and supermaxicopter.

When Tomas asked his big cousin about Giampi Super-maxihero, his cousin, his eyes glowing with nostalgia like a child's, cried, "Giampi Supermaxihero!" and immediately came out with the character's most famous catchphrase, the one about the superhero running to save a little old lady, crying, "Quick, to the supermaximobile!" then discovering the supermaximobile had been removed for parking in the wrong place, and without missing a beat crying, "Justice can't wait. Supermaxitaxi!!!" His big cousin repeated the gag word for word, without any hesitation.

Teenagers – the natural audience for *Fast Food* – loved the Supermaxihero. On buses, in school corridors, in amusement arcades, they constantly repeated the catchphrases about the supermaxidog, the supermaxi-copter, the supermaxitaxi. This went on all the three years that *Fast Food* lasted.

Then, after a slow but inexorable fall in the ratings, the show was cancelled.

For a while Francesca's father lived on his savings. He recycled Giampi Supermaxihero on Sunday afternoon family programmes, and tried to revive the narcoleptic lorry driver and the kleptomaniac traffic policeman, as well as introducing a few new characters.

But little by little, the TV appearances became less frequent. The club appearances, those little acts he put on in his purple-and-orange costume based on sketches from *Fast Food*, dried up completely.

The Supermaxihero became restless and irritable, con-stantly complaining. "How can I write comedy material when the kid's always around?" he would scream at his wife. "Here I am, trying to write things that'll make people laugh, for fuck's sake, how can I write things that'll make people laugh with the kid always under my feet, daddy this and daddy that, can't you understand I have to work, another lean year like this and my career is ruined for ever and it's all up for me, for you, for the kid, for our nice house, so will you get the kid out of my way, just get her out of my way, please, PLEASE, FOR FUCK'S SAKE?"

Then there was the drinking – the drinking and the poker. Often, dramatically, both together.

Until that terrible night when everything came to an end. The poker game with those three well-known comedians who always appeared in unpretentious Christmas movies full of belly laughs. The Supermaxihero thought of them as his friends rather than his colleagues.

He came home in the middle of the night, drunk, his face as white as a sheet, whining, "I've lost everything, everything."

And the three stalwarts of Christmas TV suddenly turned into collectors for the Mafia. They started to put pressure on the Supermaxihero, demanding their money, harassing him with threatening phone calls. He invoked their old friendship, pleaded that he was going through a bad patch, tried to get them to agree to hold off for a while, or let him pay in instalments, but they wanted their money, all of it, right now.

Francesca and her family had to move to an apartment block in the most working-class district of the city. And the reason they had to move was quite simply that the three comedians had divided up their house between the three of them.

One evening, at a birthday party at the end of middle school, Francesca watched a video with some of her class-mates. They all laughed fit to burst at that film, a box-office smash, and the range of double entendres, falls, grimaces and catchphrases demonstrated by those three well-known comedians.

57

And as Francesca watched the three of them, she remembered certain merciless phone calls, certain threats. "We'll break your thumbs", "We'll kill your daughter". Things like that.

And her friends laughed, red in the face, doubled up, with their hands on their stomachs.

It was as a result of being forced to move house, Francesca told Tomas, that her mother had her first nervous breakdown. The first, but not the last.

Her family became a time bomb. Her mother was capable of waking up in the middle of the night and screaming insults at the Supermaxihero, or bursting into Francesca's room at four in the morning, turning on all the lights and screaming, "It's your fault! It's all your fault! I should have thrown you out! I should have thrown you out!"

There were truces, but Francesca knew they could be broken on the smallest pretext. The washing machine leaking. The microwave developing a fault.

It only took a trifle to set off the timer ticking away somewhere in that apartment.

Then it was Tomas's turn, at that first meeting, to match her confidences.

He told her about his parents, who worked in a bank, and about their mellow, smiling tyranny, the way they accepted and tolerated everything, the long hair, the tattoo, the piercing, without the slightest problem.

With that little new age smile of theirs. With that look that seemed to say, "Yes, all right, you're young, you're idealistic, get all the piercings you want, cover yourself with tattoos, it makes no difference, your fate has been sealed since the day you were born, you're destined to become like us, look how happy we are, we don't need to force you to do anything, we don't need to scream at you, we're not those kinds of parents, we know how things are, you'll finish school and enrol on an economics and business studies course, you'll be a big hit with the first-year girl students because of your generally alternative look, you'll graduate with a good grade, not necessarily the top grade, but a good grade, you'll pretend to take up some creative career, a guitarist, a comic book artist, and to support yourself you'll start to do a few temporary jobs, but not for long, you'll say, just until I can afford a new fuzzbox, and before you know it you'll find yourself moaning to your friends in the pub about having to get up in the morning and how tired you feel in the evening, but you'll realize you can't do without a salary at the end of the month, and then you'll agree to a job at our bank, the bank that's put food on our table all these years, the bank that's helped us pay off the mortgage, two more years and we'll have paid off the whole of the mortgage, you'll agree to a job at the bank, and a pleasant youthful-looking personnel manager will make a pleasant youthful-sounding speech, saying, 'Just between you and me, I have six tattoos under this expensive shirt, and when I leave the bank I'm another person, I get on my motorbike in my jeans and T-shirt and go to a pub and get drunk, all by myself, that's the trick, you see, when you're in here you have to disguise yourself, change your outer appearance, but only that, remember, this shirt and tie and trousers don't change one iota of

After that first encounter in Parma, communication intensified between Tomas and Francesca. Phone calls, text messages, e-mails. It had become an obsession.

They met again, sometimes in Bologna, sometimes in Parma, sometimes halfway between the two. They often talked about what a neurotic nightmare Francesca's family was, and what a gilded quicksand Tomas's. Sometimes, when they said goodbye, she would smile gently and say, "I'll talk to you tomorrow, if my mother doesn't stab me to death in my sleep tonight because the bathroom tap isn't working." She was joking. Half joking, anyway.

"One day we'll run away," he said one spring evening, as they were enjoying the long-awaited warmth in the Parco Ducale. "One day we'll run away to London, do you like London?"

She smiled. "Why not Amsterdam?"

"We can go to London, then Amsterdam," he said.

"How about Paris?" she said. "What's wrong with Paris?"

"We can go to Amsterdam, London and Paris," he said. "Then from London we can go to Mexico, we'll find some peyote in Mexico, and we'll never come back, never, yes, one day, one day we'll run away."

One time, having contrived to skip school, they lay on the beach looking up at the sky and told each other about their phobias.

Tomas had started by talking about his attacks of vertigo. He told her about the summer he'd spent in Ireland

61

learning English, and how they'd gone on an excursion to the cliffs of Bunglass, and just approaching the edge of those cliffs with their sheer drop to the sea he'd started shaking with terror, his face had gone white and his legs weak, in the kind of panic attack he'd never before experienced in his life.

Francesca sat up abruptly, one elbow on the sand, wide-eyed. "Oh, my God," she said. "The same thing happened to me, the very same thing, when I was watching a documentary about cliffs."

That was when Tomas came out with his theories about reincarnation. They started fantasizing, inventing a story to explain the fact that they both had a phobia about cliffs. In another life, they conjectured as they lay on the beach, Francesca had been the wife of a rich old landowner, and Tomas a handsome shepherd. The old man had caught them together, and had forced them to jump off a cliff.

"Or better still," Tomas said, caught up in the game now, "the old man had us followed by his henchmen, we ran towards the cliffs, and with the ocean in front of us and those bastards behind us we did a Thelma and Louise and jumped, hand in hand."

Francesca nodded in agreement, staring up at the clouds. Then she turned and gave him an ironic look. "And who says I was the rich landowner's wife and you were the handsome shepherd? Maybe in that other life *I* was the handsome shepherd, and *you* were the rich landowner's wife."

"That's all right with me," Tomas said.

Francesca laughed. "Slut."

"Pig," he replied.

That convinced him.

Just as he had lost touch with Lisa Limone on the last day of elementary school and had met up with her again five years later on a banquette under the strobe lights, so he had left Francesca when they had hit the water, after they had jumped hand in hand from the cliff, and had found her again after an indeterminate number of cycles of life, death and rebirth, behind the bar in a pub in Parma. Wearing a *Matrix* T-shirt, the day a cover band called Red Mosquito was playing. There was no other explanation. That was how it was. It had to be.

Tomas darts through the little streets which are all named after presidents, on his legendary orange Vespa. With the words of *Thunder Road* in his head, those words Francesca had really liked. Especially the last words, underlined and highlighted in yellow.

It's a town full of losers, said the last phrase, which Francesca liked so much.

It's a town full of losers, and I'm pulling out of here to win.

The orange Vespa turns the corner of the closed shopping centre. He avoids a blue Transit van parked half on the pavement and half in the road and finds a space between the two identical white tower blocks that dominate the deserted, silent neighbourhood.

With the orange Vespa, it was a case of love at first sight. The kind you get on the first day of spring, when Bologna has thawed out after a long winter. It was then that he saw it sitting there, abandoned, under the arcade on the Via del Borgo.

That morning, he'd skipped school and holed himself up in a shop selling second-hand musical instruments. Gazing at the Fenders and the Gibsons and the acoustics, all the beautiful guitars he couldn't afford.

Tomas had so many ideas for songs in his head. He often scribbled them down in his school homework books. One day he'd be able to afford a Fender, or a Gibson, or a Takamine acoustic, and he'd form a group, a fantastic, seminal, legendary group.

Imagining himself on stage setting an audience alight with his brilliant riffs, he crossed the Via del Borgo. In the jeans shop opposite there was a cheap hat which looked as if it was crying out to be on the head of an aspiring guitar prodigy.

That was when he saw the orange Vespa. Under the portico.

Two weeks later, he went back to the second-hand instruments shop, gazed again at the Fenders and the Gibsons, and then crossed the road. The orange Vespa was still there, in exactly the same position.

Unable to resist, he went into the jeans shop.

The assistant was wearing a Carcass T-shirt, reading a grindcore magazine and sucking a lollipop, with his feet up on the cash desk. "Excuse me," Tomas said. "You don't know who that Vespa outside belongs to, do you? It's been there for two weeks. Do you know if the owner is planning to sell it?"

The assistant took the half-finished lollipop out of his

mouth and laughed. "Two weeks? That Vespa's been there for a year, even the police have lost interest in it, the bastards are always cracking down on mopeds, always handing out fines, but they don't even look at that Vespa any more."

"But what about the owner?" Tomas insisted. "Does anyone know who the owner is?"

The assistant laughed again, and looked around. The shop was empty, no one was listening.

"Look," he said in a low voice, "in my opinion, either it's stolen or the owner kicked the bucket, who knows? If I were you I'd come back at night with a hacksaw and take it away, take off the licence plate, maybe you have a friend who's a mechanic . . ."

And he went back to reading his grindcore magazine, with his lollipop in his mouth and his feet on the cash desk.

That night, at five o'clock in the morning, Tomas appeared in the Via del Borgo like a ghost. With his friend, a mechanic, equipped with all the tools of the trade.

A few days in his friend's machine shop, and the little orange Vespa was as good as new.

The little orange Vespa drives down the ramp into the garage. Into the dark belly of the white tower block.

Beneath twenty floors scorched by the sun.

Things started to move quickly one night at the beginning of August, when the rope broke, the elastic snapped, and he and Francesca took the plunge from the rock. There was no turning back. They had no other choice but to meet the ocean together, locked in an embrace, far from everything, far from everyone.

Tomas always slept with his mobile switched on next to his pillow, ready to answer Francesca's messages or calls.

That night she phoned him at two-thirty sounding distraught and desperate.

Startled out of a deep sleep, it took Tomas a few moments to make out what she was saying through her tears.

"I've had enough, I've had enough," Francesca was saying. "I'm going to throw myself out of the window, I'm going to throw myself out of the window . . . I've had enough, I can't stand it any more."

Tomas sprang to a sitting position on the bed. Electricity snaked down his spine, making the hair on his back stand up.

"Calm down," he started repeating like a broken tape, "calm down, calm down, I'm coming there now, I'm coming there, wait for me, I'll get dressed and get on my Vespa, I'll take a train, I'm coming to Parma, calm down, calm down." But she kept sobbing, "No, no, I'm throwing myself out of the window, then it'll all be over, I'm throwing myself out of the window and it'll all be over, I can't stand it any more." And he kept saying, "No, no, I'm coming over there, calm down, calm down, I'm coming over there." And she just repeated, "I've had enough, I can't stand it any more."

In the end, there was no need for him to get on his Vespa or take a train, no need to go all the way to Francesca's.

They just needed to stay connected all night, distant and yet close, each clinging to the other's voice, letting the shadows disperse, waiting together for the sun.

He even managed to make her laugh, around five in the morning. True, the laughter was mixed with tears, but all the same the worst was over. For that night at least, night had turned into day.

But the rope had broken, the elastic had snapped, once and for all.

And Tomas and Francesca started to plan their escape.

These two lanes will take us anywhere, that Bruce Springsteen song said, the one Tomas's big cousin had introduced him to. *Come take my hand . . . sit tight, take hold,* the song said.

Get away, they had to get away, *It's a death trap,* that other song said, *this town rips the bones from your back . . . some day, girl, I don't know when, we're gonna get to that place where we really want to go, and we'll walk in the sun,* it said, *but till then, tramps like us, baby, we were born to run,* to get away, to get away, to escape, to go far, far away.

August Bank Holiday Sunday, they decided. August Bank Holiday Sunday was perfect.

Tomas's parents were at a new age summer school, doing a self-development course, the climax of which would be a walk on hot coals. They wouldn't be back before Tuesday.

Tomas would leave a note before going, in which he would apologize for stealing money from the drawer, among other things. His parents would understand, they might even forgive him. Especially as they'd be full of good vibes after the summer school and a walk on hot coals.

67

As for Francesca's parents, that evening they were going to dinner with the ex-Supermaxihero's brother. Ostensibly to patch things up in a relationship that had been quite strained in the past few years. The real purpose was to ask for a loan – Francesca's uncle owned two restaurants and was about to open a third.

It was a perfect plan.

Tomas would take the eight o'clock intercity train. At eight fifty-four he would get off at Parma, where Francesca would be waiting for him. Together, they'd catch the 9:25 train, the train that would take them far away.

Francesca would also leave a note for her parents. They would find it when they got back from their dinner with her uncle, after being refused a loan – there was no doubt about that – feeling edgy and embittered. One more reason to get away, to escape, even if they didn't have much money, even if they didn't have a goal. Once they were far enough away from the poison that was killing them both in different ways, they would find a place to go.

Tomas leaves the Vespa in the garage. He's about to close the door, but then stops.

He might not see his Vespa again for quite a while. In fact, he might never see it again.

He's decided to take a bus to the station. Or even walk. He has no intention of abandoning his orange Vespa to its destiny, leaving it to die outside the station. Better to take the bus, even if it takes forever to come because it's summer. Or walk for an hour and a half in this heat.

He can't stand the idea of waiting all those hours at

home until it's time to catch the eight o'clock train. He could easily leave here long before he needs to, and walk to the station, with his rucksack on his back. Anything, just to shorten the wait.

He sighs and looks at his legendary Vespa for what may be the last time.

He goes back inside the garage, caresses the orange-coloured frame, and says, "Bye, old girl, behave yourself, don't do anything I wouldn't do."

Then, slowly and rather sadly, he closes the door.

He climbs the stone stairs that lead to the entrance hall, thinking about Francesca's delightfully asymmetrical face, and how beautiful she'll be when she gets on the train at Parma station.

At that thought, it's as if his feet leave the ground.

Because today is the most important day of his life. He has just a few hours' wait, a few hours to spend as best he can.

In his euphoria, he's about to float all the way to the elevator when, out of the corner of his eye, he sees a girl standing outside the main door, fiddling with her keys. She's wearing a barmaid's uniform or something like that. He knows her, she's the girl on the nineteenth floor, the one with the tiny mouth and huge eyes. The one his mother is a hundred per cent certain is a lesbian.

Tomas is about to keep walking, but he's feeling so happy, so light-hearted, he decides to be a gentleman. He opens the door for her.

And smiles.

* * *

Tomas hates being in an elevator with strangers. He's on the point of going to the stairs and walking up, but then thinks better of it. *The girl will think I'm rude and don't want to keep her company, how would that make me look?* he wonders, full of warm vibes, a perfect little gentleman.

So he stands there with the supposed lesbian, waiting. *A few seconds in an elevator,* he thinks. *What's the big deal?*

They're waiting for the elevator, he and the likely lesbian with the green hair, when the main door opens again and vomits up a guy with ridiculous sideburns.

The man mumbles a laboured, reluctant "Hello", and also starts waiting.

The elevator arrives. The doors open.

Tomas continues to play the gentleman. Soon he'll be seeing his old life in the rear-view mirror, getting smaller and smaller, and he's full of adrenalin, he feels happy.

He lets the girl go in first, and walks in after her, followed by the man with the ridiculous sideburns.

The doors close.

The elevator starts to ascend.

Zero Hour

The elevator is a Skylark 2000. Maximum weight 1,000 pounds, maximum capacity six persons.

The walls of the elevator are of satinized stainless steel.

The elevator has just passed the first floor.

Claudia pretends to search for her keys. Her throat feels like flypaper, she can't stand this heat any more, this viscous heat that burns the lungs.

As soon as she gets home, she'll rush to the kitchen, open the fridge, pour herself a glass of ice-cold water and drink it down in one go. Then she'll refill the glass, this time with iced tea. She'll drink that in one go too.

Once she's dealt with that first priority – quenching her thirst – she'll finally be able to take off her uniform. Then she'll spend half an hour in the shower. She's sweaty, her clothes are sticking to her, she can't wait to feel the water on her skin.

After the shower, she'll check her e-mail. Maybe Bea has found ten minutes to write to her from Morocco. Maybe.

A few more seconds and Claudia will be home.

In the meantime she's pretending to search for her keys, as she always does when she doesn't want to meet people's eyes in the elevator.

The elevator has just passed the second floor.

* * *

The Skylark 2000 has a system of indirect overhead
lighting.

The light comes from fluorescent tubes, with a plexiglas
diffuser in the push-button control panel.

The control panel is made of metal laminated in
plastic.

The elevator has just passed the third floor.

Tomas is pretending to read the metal plate on the wall
opposite the control panel.

He's pretending to study the technical data about the
elevator's maximum weight and capacity, thinking all
the while, *A sweater, I should pack a sweater, God knows where
Francesca and I will be this winter, maybe in London. Of course
in summer, when you live in a furnace like Bologna over August
Bank Holiday, cold is an abstract concept, but you have to
plan ahead*, Tomas thinks, while pretending to read the
metal plate and the technical data about weight and capacity.

Tomas has never been to England, but he has a clear
memory of the weather in Ireland, the drizzle, the
dampness. He was always half-ill in Ireland, with a runny
nose and an itchy throat. *Where is the sweater? Where does
my mother keep the winter clothes?* he wonders. *A watch too.
I ought to take a watch.* Tomas never wears a watch, but he
has a train to catch and he has to keep to the timetable,
he doesn't want to risk missing the train because of his
aversion to watches.

He searches for his keys in the pocket of his jeans, just

as the girl with green hair is pretending to do an inch or two from him.

He fingers them one by one. The key to the apartment. The key to the main entrance. The key to the Vespa. The key to the garage. The long key to the basement, big and jangly in his pocket. The one Francesca joked about once, with uncommon slyness.

"It feels like something else," she laughed, staring at the bulge made by the key in his jeans.

Taken by surprise, Tomas blushed. "What?"

"Nothing," she replied, neatly skating over it, right there in the middle of the Parco Ducale on a glorious spring day.

A few more seconds and Tomas will be home. In the meantime, he's pretending to be interested in the technical data on the metal plate.

The elevator has just passed the fourth floor.

The elevator is seven feet high. The floor is made of steel covered in bubble rubber, and the ceiling is of white steel.

There are two automatic sliding doors covered in satinized stainless steel.

The elevator has just passed the fifth floor.

Ferro is staring at the thighs of the girl with green hair, which are lavishly revealed by the uniform.

Nice legs.

She's a bit short for my taste, a bit flat-chested, but she has nice legs. I know that uniform. I have a feeling she works in that bar in the centre of town, what's it called, I went there with the Dentist, what's it called, it's in the centre of town.

73

In his head, Elvis is singing *Bridge over Troubled Water* on stage in Las Vegas.

Quite different from the version by those two pansies with their thin little voices, Simon and Garfunkel. Elvis took hold of that song, chewed it up and spat it out, making it quite different from the version by those two pansies with their thin little voices. Elvis moulded that tune in his heart, shaped it in his throat and gave it back to the world, brand new and white-hot.

A few more seconds and Ferro will be in his old bachelor flat. In the meantime he's looking at the thighs of the girl with green hair.

The elevator has just passed the sixth floor.

The Skylark 2000 is three-and-a-half feet deep by three feet wide.

The Skylark 2000 has just passed the seventh floor.

Simultaneously, Tomas and Claudia find the keys to their respective apartments, separate them with their fingers from the others in the bunch. The elevator has just passed the eighth floor.

Ferro is also searching for the key to his apartment. It's right at the bottom of his pocket, next to the jack knife.

The elevator has just passed the ninth floor.

He's dying for a cigarette. He has a packet of cigarettes and a Zippo lighter in the pocket of his shirt.

As soon as I get in I'll light a cigarette. First I'll have a glass of water, because this heat is killing me and my shirt is sticking to my fucking back, and then I'll have a cigarette.

The Skylark 2000 has just passed the tenth floor.

It's 5:03 p.m., and the Skylark 2000 elevator has just passed the eleventh floor.

When, all of a sudden, the lights go out in the elevator.

And the elevator stops.

Between the eleventh and twelfth floors.

Hour One

"When it happens, it's funny and it takes you by surprise," a little voice says inside Claudia's head. "When the film tears suddenly, in the middle of a piece of dialogue, and the audience goes 'Oh!', and there's nothing left, no plot, no subplots, no twists, no characters, just a black screen.

"When it happens, it's funny and it takes you by surprise," the little voice says inside Claudia's head. "When a pair of sharp scissors cuts into the course of a life, when an 'Oh!' of pure astonishment marks a point of no return in what has been until then a logical, coherent flow of thermometers under the armpits and vaccinations and tooth braces and parties with the blinds down and gynaecologists and appendicitis, and when it's time for the scissors you realize there was no point in looking right and left before crossing, having a bath two hours after eating, avoiding dark streets, the scissors cut just the same, when it's time for the scissors.

"Do you remember Christmas Eve?" the little voice inside her head whispers. "You were sitting in the passenger seat, next to Bea, the two of you had just come out of the pizzeria, feeling merry from the wine you'd been drinking, and it was cold and drizzling hard. And it took a while for the car to get started, but eventually it did, puffing and spluttering in the late December chill. And you took the ring road, you were wearing your hippy gloves and your rough woollen scarf and the cap with the Superman badge, and there was no one on the road, absolutely no one, do you remember?

"And you switched on the radio, and they were playing an old song by Skiantos, and you started to sing along, perfectly in time with Freak Antoni's voice, and you drove up onto the ring road singing *I'm a rebel, mama, go to bed, don't stay up*, you passed the half bend halfway up the ramp, a strip of asphalt between the fields and the scrub, out there on the edge of the city. You noticed the smoke just past the half bend. Two columns of smoke in the middle of all that sleet. Two columns rising in the darkness.

"Do you remember what you thought, seeing those columns of smoke, Claudia? 'The scrub has caught fire,' you thought, 'weeds burning in the fields,' that's what you thought.

"Then you saw two shapes, through the darkness and the rain.

"And the smoke, you realized in a fraction of a second, wasn't coming from the fields or from the surface of the road. The smoke was coming from those two black things in the middle of the deserted ramp. Two dark masses right there in front of you.

"Another fraction of a second, and you saw what those black things were. They were two cars, both smashed to pieces, the headlights shattered and dead, the bonnets gone. Hard to see in the darkness.

"That was when you and Bea realized.

"The two smoking carcasses formed a barrier across the road, obstructing both lanes.

"You were bearing down on that barrier of fire-blackened metal at eighty an hour, on a wet road. With no space to get through the middle. And on either side, a guardrail and a thirty-foot drop down to the fields.

"Then you let out an 'Oh!' of pure astonishment, when you realized that there wasn't the tiniest gap you could slip through to avoid a collision. When the normal ebb and flow of a day on which events had proceeded logically, one after the other, had been cut with a pair of scissors, like two invisible carcasses on the ramp leading to a ring road. Or an elevator stuck between the eleventh and twelfth floors.

"Bea hit the brakes as hard as she could, do you remember? Her arms rigid at the wheel.

"You hadn't closed your eyes, not yet. You were deafened by the heart-rending moan of the tyres on that inferno of twisted metal and shattered windows and mirrors.

"Only when Bea swerved at the last moment, putting the car at right angles to the road in order to avoid a frontal collision, only then did you close your eyes. A moment before that dull thud as you hit the carcass.

"Then – do you remember? – you opened your eyes.

"Your car had done all it could, but it was alive, not moving but with the engine still on. It was intact, stood there in front of the two dark, silent cars. Amid spirals of smoke, beneath the sleet, between the fields and the scrub.

"Freak Antoni was still singing *I'm a rebel, mama,* while all around was silence."

When the Skylark 2000 stops, Claudia lets out an "Oh!" which could have come from the black box flight recorder of a plane dredged up from the slime at the bottom of the ocean.

The elevator suddenly goes dark. Claudia sways because of the sudden halt, moves her hands about in the darkness and instinctively clutches the shoulder of the boy with the Bruce Springsteen T-shirt. She clings on, whispering an apology.

Then a light comes on. A green light.

"Fuck!" Ferro mutters when the elevator goes dark. Instinctively, he puts his hand in his pocket, where the knife is.

The Skylark 2000 stops suddenly. There's an aftershock, a single aftershock, almost like a hiccup. Ferro staggers and opens his arms wide, looking for a support that isn't there. He presses his palms against the smooth steel walls.

The green light sweeps away the darkness.

Tomas has just remembered where his mother keeps the winter clothes. He can visualize the sweater on top of a neat pile of heavy garments, in the wardrobe in the basement. Next to the cardboard box, the big one, where his old Dylan Dog comics lie alongside his father's Tex Willer collection.

Then the elevator jolts to a halt and, from one moment to the next, turns as black as ink.

· Tomas tenses, and stares wide-eyed into the blackness.

A moment later, the emerald light dissolves the ink.

Tomas is stuck between the eleventh and twelfth floors. With a girl who has green hair and an Elvis lookalike wearing snakeskin boots.

And when the darkness gives way to that sombre green, everything starts to move very quickly. The external trappings vanish – old Sun Records recordings, Fifties Nembo Kid comics, songs scribbled on school timetables – leaving just instinct and adrenalin

(*the fear of being buried alive the fear of enclosed spaces the fear of cellars the fear of strangers invading your space breathing your air the dream of the tunnel in the mountain the dream of the tunnel in the mountain the fear of being buried alive the fear of being buried alive*)

and three rational people suddenly become mere wasps in an upturned glass.

The elevator stops shaking. Tomas looks at Ferro, Ferro looks at Claudia. Claudia looks at the green light, which comes from the plexiglas diffuser.

Tomas presses himself against the wall, the way he used to when he was a child. When they had to give him an injection, and he flattened himself in a wardrobe or under a table until his father pulled him out kicking and screaming. Now, instinctively, he moves back a couple of inches. He rests his back against the steel wall, just beneath the metal plate with details of what to do in case of emergency.

"We've stopped," he murmurs incredulously.

"Oh, no," Ferro hisses. "I don't fucking believe it, this fucking elevator."

Claudia springs round to the control panel, searches for the alarm button, and presses it twice. She turns back to the two green and black figures and says, "I pushed the alarm button," and Ferro glowers at her and says, "Yes, I saw you, this fucking elevator, I don't fucking believe it," and three people who can rattle things off from memory – one of the three every single song by Elvis Presley, another of the three every Superman series there ever was, and the third of the three every word of *Thunder Road* – have become in an instant three hearts beating wildly, as alert as wolves.

For a few moments they wait in silence, breathing heavily at each other, each staring up into the air, at a different part of the elevator. They're waiting for the elevator to start up again. Or for someone to hear the alarm and get them out of here. They are three wasps in an upturned glass, and the upturned glass measures three-and-a-half feet by three feet. They are consuming each other's air, in the upturned glass.

Ferro curses, takes his mobile out of his pocket, shoves Tomas aside, and reads the metal plate behind him. The words on the plate are *In case of emergency: 24-hour service*, followed by a number in green.

Ferro is about to dial the number. He looks down at the mobile and stops.

No network, the screen says. *No network*.

"Fucking hell," Ferro grunts. "I don't fucking believe it." He presses buttons at random on the keypad of his mobile, switches it off, switches it on again. The screen is stuck on *No network*. He looks up. "Are yours working?" he barks. "Your mobiles?"

Claudia rummages in the Peruvian bag for her orange Nokia. She purses her lips. "There's no reception," she says, very slowly. "Mine doesn't have any reception."

"Neither does mine," Tomas says disconsolately, looking down at his unusable red and blue Ericsson. For some inexplicable reason, all three mobiles have been reduced to pieces of plastic and iron, and the 24-hour emergency service is as distant and unattainable as the moon.

In a fury, Ferro lets fly at the control panel. He presses the alarm button six consecutive times, waits a few moments, presses it a seventh time, and roars, "Fucking hell, there's no noise. Can either of you hear the alarm ringing? Shouldn't it be ringing all over the building? Shouldn't you be able to hear it all over the building?"

"Maybe it's just us who can't hear it," Tomas suggests. "Because we're shut up in here. Maybe they can hear it all right outside."

"Fucking hell, it's made specially," Ferro says bitterly. "The fucking thing's made specially to be audible. What the fuck's the point of an alarm you can't hear, for fuck's sake?"

Claudia is staring at the screen of her Nokia and that inexplicable *No network*. "To think they repaired this elevator last week," she mutters. "The maintenance men. They were here last week. Did a good job, didn't they?"

Ferro tightens his grip on his mobile. He feels like a wolf caught in a trap, a wolf determined to get free, pulling and scratching, biting through his own paw if he has to. He swears under his breath, then something occurs to him.

He remembers something he's seen on TV, one of those programmes his wife likes so much, *Last Minute* or something like that. He remembers an item about an elevator, a married couple who were stuck in an elevator.

Wait, concentrate, try to remember. Why were those two losers stuck in an elevator? What was the cause of the breakdown?

Rust?

A button that's not often used, right? It was a button that's not often used, and it had rusted and created a faulty connection, wasn't that it? That was the button those people pressed, right? That was the button they pressed and the elevator immediately started up again, wasn't that it?

A button that's not often used, a button that's not often used, what's a button that's not often used? The Stop button! Fuck, the Stop button!

Triumphantly, he presses the Stop button once, twice, ten times, fifteen times, then another fifteen times, while Tomas and Claudia watch. The elevator doesn't move.

Ferro takes a deep breath and stares hard at the control panel as if he wants to burn through it with the heat from his eyes.

Wait, keep calm, think about that programme, wait, try to remember. There was an expert in the studio, Gloria made a comment about his ridiculous beard, try to remember. The expert had advice about what to do if you were trapped in an elevator, he said you should press a button for one of the floors, a button at one of the two ends, the ground floor or the last floor. There was a technical reason for that. I can't remember what it was. Who gives a fuck?

So he presses the button for the ground floor ten times.

Then the twentieth floor ten times.

The elevator doesn't move.

Ferro loses patience. He punches the steel wall and

84

screams, "Fucking hell! Fuck! Fuck!" and his voice echoes in that coffin of dead metal as if they were deep in a crypt. His eyes dart all over the place, searching for some kind of gap or crack, a way out. He shoots a glance at the other two – useless bodies consuming air and occupying space – and then focuses on the closed doors.

There's something not right about these doors. What is it?

Use your head, man, use your head. It's obvious.

They should be open.

There must be a photoelectric cell. If the current goes off, the photoelectric cell stops working. There's nothing to keep these two doors closed.

Maybe, just maybe, we were lucky and we stopped at a floor. Maybe the doors to the floor are just behind there, maybe we can open them from the inside and wriggle out.

He puts the backs of his hands together and sinks his fingers into the intersection between the doors. He tries to open them, pulling in both directions. The doors don't even move a fraction of an inch.

He grits his teeth and turns to Tomas.

"You!" he orders. "Help me!"

Tomas obeys mechanically, rubbing involuntarily against Claudia as he dashes forward. They are like worms trapped in a jar, they can't avoid brushing against each other with every movement they make and stealing each other's air.

Ferro and Tomas take up positions opposite each other, Tomas at the door on the left, Ferro at the door on the right. They try to get a grip on the steel, but their fingers are sticky and sweaty and keep slipping. They dig their nails into the intersection, trying to push their fingertips in as far as they will go. Claudia leans forward to help them, but there's no room to move in the three feet of the elevator's width. The two backs – Ferro's broad and massive and Tomas's thin and bony – don't leave the tiniest bit of space for her to squeeze into and help the battle of flesh against metal.

Ferro and Tomas struggle a bit more, then Tomas has an idea.

"Wait," he says. "Let's use this."

He searches in his pocket for the key to the basement, the big, heavy, solid one. He uses it like a wedge, inserting it between the two doors and trying to lever them open. After much sweating and gasping, the two doors finally move an inch or so apart.

That's all they need.

Ferro's and Tomas's fingers start to invade that narrow gap, pushing, pulling, widening the gap. They make one final effort, and at last, after all that resistance, the doors yield and open.

In front of them there's a wall.

The wall of the elevator shaft, solid and impregnable. Between the elevator shaft and the elevator, there's a gap of just three miserable inches.

"Shit," Tomas murmurs.

Ferro sighs. "Great. All that effort for nothing. We've done a great job. Oh, yes, a great job."

He lets go. His door moves back along the runner to its original position.

Tomas also lets go, and the two doors meet up again in the middle with a dull, metallic thud.

It doesn't make sense. Automatic doors never work like that, as if they had springs. They work by photoelectric cell, they work by current. Fuck. It really doesn't make sense.

86

He gives up trying to understand, and looks hopefully at the screen of his mobile. But all he sees are the same two words, *No network*, and he repeats them like a mantra . . . no network, no network, no network . . . and inhales the small amount of red-hot air that's in the elevator. He breathes in and out, trying to calm down.

He breathes in.

He breathes out.

He breathes in.

He breathes out.

He breathes in.

Claudia watches the doors closing again, her eyes blank, a feeling inside her poor, tired, dehydrated head like dirty water eddying away.

She is living through a day so awful it eclipses any previous awful day she's been through. Stuck here in an elevator with two strangers, sweaty and exhausted, with Bea a long way away, yes, great, isn't it? This August Bank Holiday is definitely moving high up the list of the worst days in all her twenty-four years of life.

It's already worse than a foul day in April, when the alarm clock let her down on the morning of her exam, she missed every bus she could possibly have missed, the exam was humiliatingly difficult, it started pouring with rain just as she left the faculty, the bus was stuck in a jam for forty minutes, and when she finally got home, wanting nothing more than to throw herself on the bed, go to sleep and forget everything, she realized as she stood outside the main entrance of her building that she had left her Peruvian bag in the faculty.

With her keys in it.

Even that horrible April morning, fuck, even that has been far outstripped by this wonderful August Bank Holiday afternoon. Stuck in an elevator. Mere yards from a shower and a glass of water. In the company of two complete strangers. And three mobile phones which for no reason at all have decided to take a holiday in the ionosphere.

All three of them.

Shit.

Claudia, Ferro and Tomas wait. For the elevator to start up again. Or for someone to get them out.

Frustratingly aware that there's nothing else, nothing else at all, they can do but wait.

Gradually the wasps start to move about, start to scamper expectantly up the smooth sides of the glass.

It's just a little piece of time stolen from our lives. Like a traffic jam on the motorway, no better or worse than a traffic jam on the motorway. Or a queue at the post office. Or a flat tyre. It's just a little piece of time stolen from our lives.

So the three of them calm down. They come out of the frenzied adrenalin-fuelled nightmare. They start to talk, slowly, thoughtfully. To weigh their words.

To analyse the situation.

"We still can't hear anything," Ferro mutters, pressing the alarm button ten times. "An elevator isn't isolated acoustically, is it? We should be able to hear the alarm in here, it's meant to be heard all over the building, dammit, so we should be able to hear it in here, right?"

Tomas scratches his chin, leaning against the steel

wall. "Maybe the blackout knocked it out. The alarm, I mean."

Ferro looks him up and down. "Listen, young man, I have no idea how the alarm buttons work in elevators, I've never studied elevator maintenance. But" – he moves his hands like a lecturer – "thinking about it logically, surely an alarm is meant to work precisely when there's a loss of current, right? Otherwise, what the hell's the point having an alarm button in an elevator anyway?"

Claudia says nothing. Instead she checks her Nokia to see if it's come back to life. She makes a face and shoves the phone back in the Peruvian bag.

For a few moments no one says a word. Not Ferro, not Claudia, not Tomas. They are waiting for the situation to go back to normal, for the cables and counterweights to start working again, for the elevator to move.

They breathe impatiently over one another, in this cubby-hole three and a half feet deep and three feet wide, beneath the metal plate that says *Maximum weight 1,000 pounds, maximum capacity six persons,* and the unusable 24-hour emergency number, with a floor of bubble rubber under their feet and a white ceiling over their heads. And the green light all around them, as if they were in a submarine, crushed by the merciless pressure of the ocean bed.

Each master of his or her own territory. Aware of everything in his or her own third of the space.

A territory three feet wide and not much more than a foot deep.

Ferro has taken the territory adjacent to the exit.

He is standing in front of the control panel, those bloody

doors to his left, Tomas and Claudia to his right. He's sweating like a pig with its throat cut. There are two very conspicuous dark patches under the armpits of his white shirt with its country-style embroidery. Not even that time on the intercity train with the sun beating down, no water, the air conditioning out of order, the windows stuck, not even that time on the intercity train did he suffer so much from the heat.

His wallet is in the right back pocket of his trousers.

His keys in the left front pocket.

The packet of cigarettes and the Zippo lighter in his shirt pocket.

And the jack knife in the right front pocket.

He's dying for a cigarette.

Claudia reigns over the territory in the middle. Facing her is the metal plate with the elevator's weight and capacity. Behind her, the green emergency service number.

She has turned so that the doors are on her right, and she moves as little as possible in order not to brush up against Ferro. Ferro has an unpleasant smell, a mixture of sickly-sweet scent and rancid sweat. There was also another smell underneath. Something alien and indefinable, like nothing she's ever smelled before.

She grips the strap of her Peruvian bag, which contains the unusable mobile, the keys to her apartment, and the chocolate biscuits she nibbled at on the bus.

Claudia isn't hungry. Not at all. She's quite capable of not touching food for two whole days without feeling any pangs of hunger, and then living for the next two days on nothing but biscuits, Nutella and Coca-Cola. Bea hated watching her eat.

"Even in America your eating habits would be quite unacceptable," she would say, watching her gulp down that mixture of biscuits, Nutella and Coca-Cola. "Even in the most barbarous and uncivilized state in the Midwest."

What Claudia is, is thirsty. She was thirsty before getting into the elevator, but by now the heat and the tension have made her throat, tongue and palate completely dry.

She's dying for a drink.

Tomas is crouched at the rear of the elevator, his back against the steel doors. He first tried to sit down facing the doors, but then realized he can't do that without invading Claudia's space. So he tried to sit down sideways, in the three feet of the elevator's width, his arms around his shins, but he found that such an uncomfortable position that he gave up trying to sit and moved to a crouching position. He's waiting.

Tomas isn't worried. He still has time to catch the eight o'clock train. Lots of time.

His ticket is in the pocket of his jeans. His Bruce Springsteen T-shirt is bathed in sweat.

He plays nervously with his keys.

He's dying to see Francesca.

Ferro breaks the silence.

"Let's think this through," he says, calmly, lucidly, still moving his hands constantly. "There are two possibilities."

Claudia and Tomas stir and turn to look at him. They're all ears.

"The first is that there's been a blackout. The lights have gone out in the building, or the block, or maybe even the whole city, and the elevator stopped. If that's the case, there's a whole team of engineers repairing the generating plant or whatever, and in a while the elevator will start up again and we'll get out of here. How long can a blackout last? A blackout can't last forever, can it?"

"No, it can't last forever," Tomas agrees, reassured by Ferro's convincing, down-to-earth argument. "It can't last forever."

Yes, he's right, how long can the current be off? Half an hour? An hour, OK, let's say it lasts an hour. We get out of here at six, say, and from six to eight there's plenty of time. I can get the sweater, pack my bag, and get to the station without having to rush. I'll be able to tell Francesca all about this adventure on the way to Amsterdam.

"What's the second possibility?" Claudia insists, her eyes fixed on Ferro.

"The second possibility is that the elevator has broken down. This could be a problem, especially if the alarm isn't working, and for some fucking reason, pardon my language, our mobiles aren't working . . . I mean, if it's a general blackout someone will have informed the engineers, someone will be doing something, right? If on the other hand the whole world is still turning normally, with the single exception of this delightful elevator, well, with half the population on the beaches, it could be a while before anyone realizes we're here."

Tomas is horrified. "But someone's bound to use the elevator sooner or later, aren't they? The other one's out of order, this is the only one that's usable, someone will realize that it's stopped between two floors, won't they? We're not the only people living here. There are *sixty* apartments in this building!" He pauses, out of breath, and swallows. "Maybe we should call out; they can't all be at the seaside! The cat woman on the ninth floor, for example, the cat woman on the ninth floor certainly isn't at the seaside, or anywhere else. She's always here, with all her cats and her sandbags."

"And there's that couple with the child," Claudia says. "The one on the seventh floor, do you remember?"

"The guy with the ponytail, you mean?" Tomas asks. "Him with his ponytail and weird shirt, and her with that ridiculous hair, that couple?"

"That's them, the couple who look like they've come straight from Woodstock, they've just had a baby. They won't have gone to the seaside with a newborn baby."

Ferro again seizes the reins of the conversation. "But I go for the blackout idea." He pauses. "And I'll tell you why."

He makes a fist of his right hand and raises the index finger. "First. I'm no expert on elevators, I don't know how they work, but if there was still a current we wouldn't have been able to open the door with our hands. There must be a photoelectric cell or something like that, how should I fucking know, pardon my language, there must be a photoelectric cell that keeps them closed. Without a current the photoelectric cell doesn't work." He raises his middle finger and places it beside the index finger. "Second. The green light. As soon as the elevator stopped we were in the dark for a moment, right? And then this green light came on. Like I said, I'm no expert on elevators, but I assume it's the emergency lighting. Which comes on if there's a blackout. What do you think? Does my theory hang together?"

"There's something that isn't right," Claudia says, thinking aloud. "The doors. If there's a photoelectric cell that keeps them closed, and the photoelectric cell was put out of action in the blackout, then there's nothing to keep them closed, right? And yet as soon as you let go they went back together. As if there was a magnet or something like that, you know what I mean? What's the explanation for that?"

Ferro opens his arms wide. "Like I said, signorina, I haven't studied elevator maintenance. I can't explain why these strange doors sprang back like that either, I have the same doubts you do. But that's the way it is. Let's just bear it in mind."

Claudia raises an eyebrow. *Signorina? Did he call me signorina? Has he been doing an etiquette course or is it some weird kind of advance?*

Is that his way of coming on to me?

He's certainly got the pig face for it.

Signorina. Huh!

"I'd try calling out," Tomas insists. "There's the cat woman, there's the couple with the baby, we can't be the only three people in the building, can we?"

"That would be bad luck," Ferro jokes. All three laugh nervously.

Tomas looks hopefully at Ferro, the self-appointed organizer of the prisoners of the Skylark 2000. "So, shall we call out?"

Ferro gives him the authorization. "On three. One. Two. Three."

And on three, a collective "Ohhhh!" erupts, echoing between the steel walls, followed by a few individual cries.

Claudia shouts, "We're in here!"

Tomas yells, "Is there anybody there?"

Ferro coordinates them. "Again, all together. One, Two. Three."

They let out two more perfectly synchronized collective "OHHH"s.

Then they go back to waiting, in silence.

5:39 p.m.

Ferro leans back against the stainless steel wall, the doors to his left, the control panel facing him. His arms are folded, his eyes fixed on the tips of his shoes. He is thinking.

Let's think this through. Let's be calm and think this through.

This is one of those situations that can keep you in limbo for an indefinite period of time, but can also return to normal quite suddenly, without warning. One moment, you're cursing because the intercity train isn't moving, the sun is beating down, the air conditioning isn't working, the windows are stuck, there's no water and you feel as if you're in the last circle of hell. The next moment, the train comes back to life and sets off again, and all that frustration because you couldn't move becomes a vague memory.

Maybe in a minute we'll move, this aquarium green will turn back into the usual white light you get in elevators, and these forty minutes when our lives are suspended will just have been a trivial nuisance.

But let's be realistic.

It may be that the situation won't return to normal all that soon. You should at least consider the possibility. You could spend a whole hour, or even two, in this fucking elevator. With the mobiles gone haywire. With an alarm which probably doesn't work. With the elusive cat woman and the equally elusive hippy couple who can't hear us calling out.

And no one, not a single fucking person in the last forty minutes, has realized that there's an elevator stuck between two floors.

So let's be realistic about this. We may get out of here in the next minute, but in the meantime let's make the best of a bad job. What was it the Dentist used to say? Turn dross to gold.

The girl is short and flat-chested, agreed. She's not exactly pretty, with that bristly green hair, that thin face like a lynx. But her legs aren't bad at all. And she's wearing the kind of outfit that could get a girl raped in the park.

All right then, fuck it, let's turn dross to gold!

It's show time!

Ferro puts on a sardonic, confident little smile. He looks at Tomas, who's motionless and silent, pressed up against the wall on the other side of the elevator. In between them, Claudia is trying to sit down along the width of the elevator, wedging her legs into the small amount of space at her disposal.

"Nice T-shirt," Ferro observes, speaking very slowly. "You like Bruce Springsteen, do you? Is he your idol, your favourite singer?"

Tomas stirs himself and looks up. "Yes. Well actually, I like *Born to Run*."

Ferro scratches his thigh, just below where the jack knife sits at the bottom of his pocket. "He's an OK guy, Bruce Springsteen. He's someone who knows the difference between the master and the pupil. Do you know who my favourite singer is?"

"Elvis," Claudia cuts in, her arms around her knees. "Just a guess."

Ferro smiles. "Of course. And do you know how many Elvis songs Bruce Springsteen has covered? Lots of them. *Good Rockin' Tonight. Viva Las Vegas. Can't Help Falling in Love. Follow that Dream* . . . I collect every cover version of Elvis's songs, every single one, even the most disrespectful and degrading. Your Bruce Springsteen doesn't have a voice like Elvis, of course, no one has a voice like Elvis, but it's obvious he sings those songs with respect. I like to see respect shown to a master. Did you know Bruce Springsteen once climbed over the gates of Graceland to meet Elvis?"

"No, I didn't know that," Tomas admits, and all the while he's thinking, *This is weird. Really weird. We're making conversation as if we were in the queue at the post office, we're talking about our musical idols instead of calling out or trying to find a way to get out of here. Fuck this, I've got a train to catch at eight o'clock.*

Ferro laughs. "I knew it and you didn't. All right, then, let me tell you the story. Your friend Bruce climbed the gates of Graceland to meet Elvis. He was stopped by a guard, and had to explain to him, you know, who he was and what he wanted. He was already famous, but he didn't mind being treated like any other troublesome fan just to meet his idol. That's why I respect your friend Bruce." Then he changed tone, becoming quite professorial. "If I ever have a son, I'll never let him grow up listening to the pre-packaged crap they play on the radio. If I ever have a son, I'll make him listen to the King. I'll make sure he grows up with good music."

"Don't you have any children?" Claudia asks.

Proudly, Ferro displays the ring finger of his left hand. "No children. No wife. No ring." The fact is, he took off the ring when he was in the car, on his way to make his play for the barmaid from the Pink Cadillac. "I'm as free as a bird. I like to enjoy life, without anything to tie me down." Then, to cover all the bases, he adds, "But in my heart, I'm always ready for love. I fall in love every day, on the bus, in bars, in the street. Maybe one day I'll meet Miss Right."

And he celebrates this heap of bullshit by taking a cigarette from the packet. He's just put it between his lips when he sees the stern look Claudia's giving him.

"I'm sorry," she says, in a clear voice. "I don't think it's a good idea to smoke in here. There's no air." Adding mentally, *Stupid idiot.*

Ferro looks her up and down with an inscrutable expression, the cigarette still between his lips. Then he gives in. "You're right. It's not a good idea." He puts the cigarette back in the packet, and the packet in his shirt pocket.

That's all we needed, Claudia thinks. *We can't breathe as it is, there's no air, the bloody heat is killing us. I'd also like to smoke, dammit, being in here makes me want to start smoking again. I've only just quit, and now here I am, stuck in this elevator, and I could really do with a cigarette. A glass of water and a cigarette. I'm like that character in* Airplane!, *the one who says, "Looks like I picked the wrong week to quit smoking." Fuck.*

Ferro quickly regains control, after the slip he made with the cigarette. He has to ride the tiger, keep all the attention on himself.

"Did I tell you I own three clubs?" he says, talking

nineteen to the dozen. "Three clubs the King would have liked, oh yes. We've had to make a few concessions to the barbaric tastes of the day, of course; when you've invested money you expect a return, obviously, we're not a charity, we give the masses the music they like, a bit of commercial dance music, a bit of Latin American, people go to these clubs for entertainment. But there's always some personal touch, some little bit of class. Have either of you ever been to the Pink Cadillac?"

Tomas thinks about it, and says dubiously, "Once, I think."

"Well, that's one of mine. You really should go, there's a pink swimming pool shaped like a Cadillac, we fill it with foam and people dance in it. They really go crazy. It's quite the rage, dancing in foam. In September we reopen the Graceland and the Memphis. We get going in earnest after the summer break, we have lots of ideas. By the way, let me introduce myself, Aldo Ferro."

"Tomas."

"Claudia."

"Claudia," Ferro repeats, taking a deft peek down her cleavage. "Where do they wear those uniforms? What's the name of that bar, the one right in the centre of town?"

He went there with the Dentist, he's sure of it. They sat down at a corner table for an aperitif, and as they sipped their drinks the Dentist mentioned the name of a very famous record producer. He listed some records this famous producer had been responsible for, all disgustingly famous, commercial records.

Then the Dentist lowered his voice. "You know something?" he whispered. "He also makes his own films."

"The record producer?" Ferro said in surprise.

"Yes," the Dentist said, with a derisive smile. "He's too scared to go all the way, though, he shoots them in his own house and only with consenting actors." He finished his aperitif, and laughed. "He may be scared, but his wife's a total whore. They even say she has a Dobermann that's been well trained. *Very* well trained."

They both burst into coarse laughter, and continued with some quite vicious comments on the barmaids' costumes. Then they complimented the owner of the bar, what was it called? The Vivandiere, that was it, the Vivandiere.

"Do you work at Enzo's, Claudia? I know Enzo. That is where you work, right?"

Instinctively, Claudia shudders.

The Pig. Thanks for reminding me that the Pig exists. As if the day wasn't awful enough already.

"Yes," she replies through gritted teeth. "Just for the summer. To pay my tuition fees."

"He's a great guy, Enzo. Say hello to him for me."

Claudia's mouth curls in an attempt to hold back a grimace of disgust. "I will."

"I used to go to the Vivandiere with a friend of mine. He's dead now. Nasty business. We really liked the barmaids' uniforms." He winks at Tomas, in an automatic gesture of male solidarity. "The eye needs something to keep it busy too, and old Enzo knew that, how to please the customer's eye. Yes, a great guy, old Enzo."

"Right," Claudia mutters, grim-faced.

"If I were your boyfriend," Ferro says, his unpleasant, sinister voice echoing between the sweat-drenched walls, "if I were your boyfriend, I'd never let you walk around in that uniform. I'd double lock the doors at home, rather than send you out like that."

Claudia raises an eyebrow. She takes a while to work out a reasoned and not too obviously angry reply, and finally hisses, "I only work there, and I have to wear this thing. And I don't give anyone any reason to be jealous. In any situation."

Neutral, precise. Good. He's not a customer. You can even afford to be a little rude, if you want. Fuck him.

"You've got to be joking," Ferro insists. "If I were your boyfriend, I wouldn't let you walk around half naked. That's for sure." The sombre green light etches strange shadows on his face. He's breathing heavily now, like a bear.

Claudia articulates the words clearly, curtly. "There's no reason. To be. Jealous." After a pause, she adds, "No reason at all."

Tomas is at the back of the elevator, less than two feet from Ferro and a couple of inches from Claudia, an onlooker to this exchange, which leaves him slightly anxious.

He has the feeling the walls are closing in on him. They seem so near, so narrow. He closes his eyes and tries to think about something else, Francesca, Amsterdam, whatever.

Ferro looks Claudia up and down, stony-faced.

For what seems like a very long time.

Then the tension in his face relaxes, the shadows dissolve in the soft green light. He raises his hands in a sign of surrender and sneers, "OK, OK, you win."

Then he falls silent and leans against the doors.

Stay calm, stay calm, control yourself. There are priorities, remember the priorities.

101

There wouldn't be any problem if she and I were alone in the elevator. Me and the girl with green hair. That would be perfect, I'd do her right here in this elevator, standing up. Tension always makes the bitches more excited.

I wouldn't have any problems, I'm still psyched up, even that hat-trick with Sonja hasn't knocked me out. Forty years of glory, always ready, fully loaded and raring to go. Not like all the little nerds you see these days. Like this boy with his piercing, with that puny physique of his, can you imagine him trying to give himself a handjob, he'd faint. Loser says he's a fan of Bruce Springsteen, and he didn't even know the story about Graceland. Pah!

I'd like to see how he'd manage with a girl like Sonja. Wouldn't even know what to do. She'd eat him for breakfast.

If the girl and I were alone in the elevator, there wouldn't be any problems. That's for sure.

But we have this loser here with us.

And I have to behave myself.

I can't even pull out the knife in here. When they come and get us out of here, I need to leave this elevator a blameless citizen, an anonymous neighbour. I can't disgrace myself, I don't want them investigating what's in my apartment. Not even my wife knows I have an apartment in this building, and I'd like it to stay that way.

I need to be upright, clean, blameless. Just someone who had the bad luck to be stuck in an elevator for an hour or two; that's nothing, you don't get in the papers or the TV news for something like that. So I really can't use the knife.

And anyway, I wouldn't like that, having to use my knife to force her to give in to me. Aldo Ferro has never needed a knife to get a woman.

If the worst comes to the worst, and this situation goes on for much longer, I can ask the boy to turn his back while the barmaid and I dance the tango.

If he wants to he can even look. It'd teach him the right way to use the tools of the trade.

Or else I could just lay the groundwork with the girl.

Then as soon as we get out of the elevator, we politely say goodbye to the boy and the barmaid is so excited she invites me to her place.

In the meantime, though, I have to keep my original idea in mind. And my original idea is to get out of here in one piece and completely blameless. Ready to get back to Alex.

Alex who's waiting patiently for me in the shack. Looking out at the world through what used to be his mouth.

"Does anyone have any water?" Ferro gasps, with his tongue hanging out as if he's about to suffocate. Tomas opens his arms wide. Claudia replies, "I only have biscuits."

Ferro laughs. "No water. Kids, if we don't get out of here fast, with this heat we'll be reduced to drinking our own urine."

"That's disgusting," Claudia says, smiling nervously, and it's quite an effort for her to pull the muscles of her face into that smile. She doesn't like Ferro, she instinctively finds him repugnant. But repugnant as he is, until help comes she has to get along with him somehow. And if she has to get along with him, she tells herself, there's no point in there being bad blood between them, no point objecting to everything he says. *If we want to get out of here,* she tells herself, *it's best to cooperate.*

That's why she makes an effort to smile at that pitiful boast about urine.

But it's a mistake.

Because Ferro interprets that slight smile as tacit encouragement. He presses on, full of himself now. "If the worst comes to the worst, we might have to drink each other's urine, but I warn you: I've done everything and tried everything in my life. If you know what I'm saying. Everything. I can't guarantee the purity of whatever comes out of my body."

Tomas's face contorts with disgust.

"I don't believe we'll have to go as far as that," Claudia says, patiently. "They'll get us out of here long before we have to drink our own urine."

Ferro laughs. "Oh, sure. Long before we have to pee in each other's mouths, if you'll pardon my language. But kids, what if, instead of that, we have to eat each other . . . you know, like in that film about the plane that came down in the Andes . . . If that happens, be kind to me. My skin is tough and I'm full of toxic substances, I have the feeling I'm stringy and indigestible, so please, don't eat me. Mind you, looking at you, young man, I think you're a bit too scrawny to fill our stomachs. And gallantry forbids us categorically to eat such a pretty girl."

"Thanks," she says, looking away. "That's reassuring. Really, really reassuring."

There's a gleam in Ferro's eyes. He's taken command of things. The situation may be absurd, but he has it under control. He has them both in the palm of his hand as if he were at the Pink Cadillac on a normal evening, with everyone dancing in the foam and his fan club propping up the bar, drinking in his every word. So he behaves just as if he were there. To keep his audience on their toes, he tells anecdotes.

"Talking about people eating each other, did you read about that cannibal in Berlin? The one who put an ad on the internet?"

"I think so," Claudia says.

"Well, if you don't know the story, I'll tell you. This cannibal put an ad on the internet. He was looking for someone willing to be eaten by him, a consenting adult, you know what I mean? And this mad guy answered the ad, incredible, I know, but he actually answered the ad. Yes, all right, he said, I'm interested, I'm willing to be eaten by you, but the cannibal wasn't satisfied with that. Oh, no, he wanted a photo of the mad guy completely naked, he wanted to be sure he liked what he was going to eat, know what I mean? And then he made him sign a consent form, something like *I the undersigned state that I am willing to be eaten*, and so on. Finally they met. They agreed to meet at the cannibal's place."

Tomas looks at him wide-eyed. "Did he eat him?"

Ferro sniffs loudly. "First they got drunk. Then they took drugs. I don't know if they also fucked, I think they did. Anyway, in the end, the cannibal castrated the mad guy with a kitchen knife. The mad guy, I should point out, was wide awake, fully conscious, and consented to it."

"All right," Claudia protests. "I think that's enough."

Ferro ignores her and continues. "I haven't finished yet. After he'd castrated him, the cannibal put the guy's cock in a pan and boiled it. And they ate it together. I swear."

"That's impossible," Claudia remarks. "A man who's just been castrated would probably be unconscious."

"Yes, that's right," Tomas says. "He'd be in pain, losing blood. It's impossible."

105

Ferro ignores Claudia's scepticism. It's Tomas he mocks for his mild protest. "What do you know about it? There are techniques for that kind of thing. In Atlantis, doctors could keep a man alive for days on end, even after they'd taken out his intestines, even after they'd reduced him to just a body without arms and legs. There are old books about the Inquisition, or about what they used to do in the Tower of London, which mention men without eyes, without a tongue, without arms or legs, and a hole where the stomach should be, who were still alive and still lucid. There are a thousand ways to keep a person conscious even after you've reduced him to a piece of meat —" But then he breaks off. Best not to get too carried away; he doesn't want to appear too much of an expert on the subject.

Claudia looks at him, puzzled and disconcerted by this rant about torture.

Fuck. This is like some cheapo horror movie, the scene where the scoutmaster tells ghost stories in the middle of the woods. Shining a torch on his own face, with the kids gathered around him, terrified.

Just before the monster emerges from the dark and eats them all, one after the other.

"Is that story even true?" she asks sceptically.

"Absolutely. The cannibal filmed the whole thing, and when the police watched the video they vomited for a whole day. Anyway, in the end the cannibal cut the guy's throat, chopped him into pieces, threw away the stringy parts, the parts he couldn't eat, and started feasting on the rest. A bit at a time. He kept the pieces in the freezer, and —"

"Can we talk about something else?" Claudia cuts in. "About the fact that we can't breathe in here, for example, the fact that there's no air?"

"Is that all?" Ferro says dismissively. "Pass me the key, young man. That big one, the one you used before."

Mechanically, Tomas hands over the basement key. Ferro wedges it in between the doors, and using the tip of his boot manages to make a small gap again.

"Do you want a hand?" Tomas asks.

"No, kid, relax and enjoy the spectacle. Just watch me. I can open both doors."

In fact, though he doesn't let on, Ferro is having to make an enormous effort. The bloody doors don't seem to want to separate. They push against his muscles like two sides of a press, trying to close again with merciless force. But Ferro doesn't want Claudia to think he's weak. Absolutely not.

So he takes a deep breath, as if he's lifting a heavy barbell at the gym, and with a final effort opens the door, triumphantly.

"There you are," he says, panting imperceptibly. "Now we can breathe. Not exactly mountain air, but at least it's something." He holds the doors open with his arms and back. Claudia and Tomas go as close as they can, and breathe in a little of that pristine oxygen filtering into the three inches between the elevator and the wall of the elevator shaft.

"Shall we try calling out again?" Tomas suggests.

Ferro nods his approval and starts to count. "One. Two. Three."

On three they call out.

Then they call out again.

Then they try again to ring the alarm.

Then they check their mobiles, which are still dead, unusable.

Ferro is standing there, straining the muscles of his arms to the utmost, his head bent forward, one door crushing his spine, the other digging into the palms of his hands. He struggles for a while with the pressure of the metal on his skin, but finally gives in. He lets the doors close again, which they do with a noisy thud. Once again, the elevator is sealed like a tomb.

He leans against the wall, making an effort not to appear tired, concealing the fact that he's gasping for breath.

These doors. These damned doors.

How the fuck do these damned doors work?

All three are enjoying the new air that has come in from outside.

No one says a word.

5:51 p.m.

Tomas's eyes are closed.

I'm going to count to five, and when I get to five the elevator will start up again.

One. Two. Three. Four.

Five.

On five he opens his eyes.

The elevator hasn't moved.

He sighs.

I'm going to count to ten, and when I get to ten the elevator will

start up again. One. Two. Three. Four. Five. Six. Seven. Eight.
Nine.

Ten.

On ten he opens his eyes. The elevator hasn't moved.

Tomas has sat down between the doors, on the runner.
He's holding the doors open with his back and his right
knee.

He's realized where Ferro went wrong. Ferro was in the
wrong position, on his feet, taking all the pressure on his
arms. Tomas is using his whole body to resist the pressure.
His head is three inches out of the elevator, his temple
resting on the concrete wall of the elevator shaft. He is
breathing that air which is as grey and sick as a dying man's
breath.

"I still don't understand this whole door business," Ferro
says, insistently. "The doors should be open."

Hearing him start again on the same old story about the
doors that keep springing back when they should be open,
Claudia finds she can't pretend to be conciliatory any more.
Ferro is getting on her nerves, making her furious, really
furious. It's an instinctive thing. She's too close to him,
she can smell him, his smell makes the hair on the back of
her neck stand on end and gives her a tingling sensation
all down her spine. She's discovering how an animal reacts
when it senses through smell that its enemy is near.

"I thought I had a daughter and instead I have a puppy,"
her mother used to joke, when Claudia would sit down
at table and know instinctively, just by sniffing, what was
in the dish. "Jesus, Claudia," she would say with a laugh,
"what do you want, it's a steak, not cat food."

109

Ferro's smell grates on her nerves. That sickly-sweet scent covering the sweat, and that other thing – cold, strange, alien – that's underneath.

So she lets fly at him, her voice shaking with anger. "Look, I'm sorry, but are you some kind of expert on elevators? Do you know exactly how a photoelectric cell works? Because you seem pretty clued up about the subject." She tries to temper the irony in her voice, and only partly succeeds.

Ferro is immediately on the defensive. He peers at her grimly and scratches his chin. "Look, *signorina*," he says, "I don't know anything at all about elevators, I've never given a damn about elevators, I know they go up and down, and that's it. I'm just trying to be logical, and logically, if there's a current, the doors can't be opened by hand. If there isn't a current, well, they shouldn't close automatically the way they're doing." He laughs. "You, young man, had better pray the elevator doesn't start up again now, suddenly, or you might find yourself half in here and half in the elevator shaft."

"Thanks for the warning. Does anyone know what time it is?"

"Ten to six," Claudia replies.

"Do you have something to do, young man? Are you in a hurry to leave?"

"Yes. I'm supposed to be meeting someone at the station in Parma. My train leaves at eight." That's all he says, because you never know. His parents live in this building, and it's not a good idea to give too much away to the neighbours. You never know. Better to keep it vague.

"We'll be out of here long before eight," Claudia says, reassuringly. "That's for sure."

Ferro laughs again, and winks at Tomas. "Is that your girlfriend in Parma? I've had a couple of girls in Parma too. Tell your girlfriend you stood her up because you were stuck in an elevator. Some of my girlfriends have swallowed worse excuses than that. Compared with me, John Belushi was an amateur, I swear."

Claudia purses her lips in a contorted grimace. Even just listening to Ferro speak bothers her now. She has to make an effort to control her violent reaction to him, a reaction so intense and primitive, it scares her. She's never had such strong feelings of repulsion for a person.

It's the situation, it's being so close to each other, without air, without water. It's the heat, the thirst. That's all it is. Nothing more.

Apart from that smell.

Shoe polish and roasted coffee.

That alien smell.

"It's strange, you know," she hisses, making an effort to control herself. "I know all the people in this building, at least by sight. I've passed them all at least once. All except you."

Ferro tenses. "So? What of it?"

"Nothing. Only, it's weird to meet for the first time like this. Don't you think it's weird?"

"It's not surprising we've never met. I'm never at home. I have my apartment here" – he was about to say bachelor apartment, but stopped himself in time – "it's on the twentieth floor, but I'm never at home. I'm always out, visiting clubs. I go abroad a lot too, I was never meant for a sedentary life. I like to travel, you know, London, Amsterdam, Paris . . ."

111

Tomas's face lights up. "Do you know people in those places? I mean, Amsterdam, London . . . ?"

"Do I know people? I know everyone in London, Paris, Amsterdam. Of course I know people. I know everyone."

"Everyone," Claudia says ironically, although no one's listening to her. "Of course. Why not? Absolutely everyone in London and Paris. It's only natural."

"It's for a trip," Tomas explains. "A trip around Europe. If anyone could put us up, my friend and me . . ."

"Ah, the girlfriend in Parma!" Ferro says, overjoyed. "Never let it be said that Aldo Ferro stood in the way of a young couple. Love is a wonderful thing! As soon as we get out of here, I'll make a few phone calls. I can fix things up for you all over Europe, anywhere you want to go. Anything to make things easier for a young couple, right, signorina?"

Signorina? Again? Why the hell are you talking like that?

Stay in your place.

You creep.

"She's not my girlfriend," Tomas stammers, red in the face. "The girl from Parma, I mean. She's just a friend." Tomas doesn't trust them. True, Claudia doesn't look like a nosy neighbour, he can't see her blabbing to his parents: "I know where your son is! He's in Holland with a girl from Parma! They arranged to meet in Parma on August Bank Holiday Sunday! He told me all about it when we were stuck in the elevator!"

No, Claudia doesn't seem like the kind of person who'd betray him, and as for Ferro, well, it doesn't look as if Ferro is ever at home. All the same, the less other people know about their plans, the better.

The pressure of the doors is becoming unbearable. Tomas tries to move his left leg, but his knees are bunched up against his chin, and he can't resist those steel monsters any more. A few more seconds, and he rolls back inside the elevator, letting the doors close again.

"I'm sorry," he says. "I couldn't manage any more."

"Don't worry," Claudia says to console him. "Next time we run out of air, I'll stand between the doors."

"Certainly not, signorina," Ferro cuts in. "We'll never allow such a pretty young lady to suffer the pressure of those two vulgar doors. I and our young lover here" – he winks at Tomas – "will divide the task between us."

The corner of Claudia's mouth lifts slightly.

Now the pig's acting the gentleman. He hopes I'll forgive him his previous remarks.

As if I hadn't noticed the excitement in his voice when he talked about his apartment. I heard the excitement in his voice, does he think I didn't?

I think he picks up Ukrainian whores in his car and takes them to that apartment. He has orgies there with his friends, pigs like him.

Maybe he keeps a complete set of whips and handcuffs there.

They wait, breathing hot, green air.

Then Ferro surrenders to the oven-like heat. Puffing, he quickly unbuttons his white shirt and takes it off. Hit by a wave of acidulous sweat, Claudia grits her teeth and tenses her fingers until the knuckles turn white. She watches him as he folds his shirt, transferring the cigarettes and the lighter to his trouser pocket, looks at his bare gym-goer's torso, the tufts of hair on his shoulders and back, watches him as he carefully places the shirt in a corner of the elevator. Then she closes her eyes so as not to see him.

"It's funny," Ferro says, when he's finished with his shirt. "I had a dream last night that predicted this."

Tomas looks up. "What was it?"

"I dreamed I was crawling through a tunnel, on my back, inside a mountain. Then the tunnel came out in the middle of a cliff with a sheer drop to the sea, thousands of feet above a stormy sea, are you with me? And while I was there looking down, examining that wall of smooth rock, I could feel something soft and repulsive coming towards me from the other end of the tunnel, like a giant worm. So there I was, with a cliff of smooth rock on one side, a giant worm on the other, it seemed real, I can tell you. I could really smell the briny air."

"And then you woke up?" Tomas asks, genuinely interested.

Ferro smiles derisively. "Of course. I always pull through somehow. I'm not so stupid as to let myself get eaten by a repulsive worm. Even in dreams, I don't let anything get the better of me."

Claudia looks at him as if to say, "Get real, you idiot." But what she says is, "What's so funny about that dream? I'd just like to know."

She's getting on her high horse again, Ferro thinks. *Why does she have to be so fucking sarcastic?* But he doesn't let her fluster him. "The claustrophobic situation. Being in a tunnel, with all those miles of mountain over my head, the rock just an inch or two from my nose. The dark narrow tunnel. A bit like us in here, don't you think? The difference being that in that situation there was no way out, whereas here we'll

114

be out soon, laughing at all this. Well, anyway, I thought it was quite similar."

Claudia smiles, revealing her teeth. "My dream was funnier, then."

"Let's hear it," Ferro challenges her.

"I dreamed I was in the desert, in Morocco, and there was nothing but dunes for miles around. Just sand and more sand. Nothing else. I was wandering aimlessly, with the sun directly overhead. I had no idea where I was going, I had no direction at all."

Ferro frowns. "What's so funny about that?"

"The fact that I was terrified by all that space." She starts laughing to herself, hysterically. "Funny, isn't it? I was terrified by all that space. All that empty space. And now we can't even stretch our legs because we're squashed like sardines in a tin. I think that's funny. I think it's very funny."

No one else laughs. After a while she stops laughing too.

Hour Two

Tomas makes his choice. "Tails."

He too has given in to the heat. He's taken off his Bruce Springsteen T-shirt and is using it to wipe the sweat from his neck and bare chest.

Claudia is burning, melting in the heat, but she has no intention at this point of taking off her barmaid's uniform. She can already feel Ferro's slimy eyes on her; if she was just in bra and panties that would really give him fertile ground. Even though her black bra and torn white panties – she never wastes time coordinating her underwear when all she has in store is a lousy day in the bar to be got through as quickly as possible – both from the bargain bins of department stores, are the least exciting Claudia can imagine. Even to the sick mind of someone like Ferro. So she puts up with the heat and curses the porn-star barmaid's uniform. She still has that sensation at the back of her neck, like sandpaper grating on her nerves. Behind her neck, and down her back.

When Tomas makes his choice, Ferro smiles like Jack Nicholson as the Joker. He winks at Claudia and tosses the coin. He watches it as it rotates in the air, almost touches the white steel ceiling, falls back into his palm. Ferro closes his fist over it. Then he opens his fingers and gives a sneering smile.

117

"Heads," he announces. "That's thirteen-nil, to me."

"You're cheating," Claudia says accusingly.

"I'm not cheating. I'm just tossing a coin and letting it fall. We've agreed that on one-euro coins *this* is heads and *this* is tails, though in my opinion, it was much easier to play with the dear old hundred-lire coin. But anyway, we've decided arbitrarily that this side is heads and this side with the little man by Michelangelo or Leonardo da Vinci or whoever the fuck it was, the side that has the little man with four arms is tails. Having agreed on these basic rules, I've won thirteen times out of thirteen. There's no trick. It could be heads, it could be tails."

"But not always heads," Tomas objects. "It's statistics."

"You want to try tossing the coin, young man? Here's my euro. Don't let it slip out of those sweaty little hands."

"My hands aren't sweaty. Heads or tails?"

"Heads. They bring me luck."

Tomas tosses the coin. He watches it fly above the metal plate, stop at the height of its trajectory, then, pulled down by the force of gravity, fall back into the palm of his hand. He stares down at it, incredulously.

"Heads," he murmurs. "It's not possible. It's really not possible."

Ferro guffaws. "Fourteen-nil. We should start playing for money."

"It's really not possible," Tomas says, giving the coin back to its owner. "It's statistics. Not an opinion. Statistics."

"Listen, young man, I don't know much about statistics, but I have a feeling the laws of statistics are out of the running at the moment. Look at the three of us."

Claudia frowns. "I don't follow you."

"Well, aren't we a statistical anomaly, the three of us? Have you been into town this afternoon? There's no one around, I mean, no one at all. This afternoon I could have left my car in the middle of the road, stretched out on the surface and taken a nap in the sun, and no one would have seen, because, quite simply, there was *no one* around." He lowers his voice, calm and persuasive now. "And then, suddenly, in this desert, the three of us pop up. In the same building. At the same moment. How many times in your lives have you ended up in an elevator with *two* strangers? With *one* stranger, OK, that's normal, but *two*? And it happens precisely on a day when the city is empty, come on, that's not normal at all. There are primal forces at work here." He strokes his coin earnestly. "Seems to me I could toss this euro another four hundred times, and it would come down heads four hundred times. The laws of probability are all mixed up today."

Claudia mutters an almost inaudible "Huh!" and makes a gesture with her hand, as if swatting away a mosquito.

Tomas changes the subject. "How long have we been in here?" he asks.

Ferro looks at his watch. "An hour and a half."

Tomas moans, imperceptibly.

Half past six.

Fuck it, I'll have to use the Vespa to get to the station. I'll have to leave the Vespa outside the station, in the sun, where it could easily get stolen. Just thinking of it breaks my heart.

Unless we get out of here now, straight away. If the elevator starts up again right now, I can still do it, I'll forget about the sweater, zoom outside like a pea from a peashooter, I might even

119

be able to get to the station on foot. If the worst comes to the worst, I hope I can find a bus. Just as long as I get on that train by eight.

If the elevator starts up again now. Right now, this moment.

If we get out of here right now.

Fuck.

Fuck.

Isn't anyone repairing those fucking generating plants?

How fucking long does it take to repair a fault?

Isn't anyone repairing those fucking generating plants?

Claudia suddenly stirs herself and leaps to her feet, her knees creaking painfully. She's had an idea, a totally logical, totally obvious idea. "What if we tried getting out through the top?"

Tomas looks at her, hopefully. "Do you think it's possible? Can we do it?"

"Why not?" Ferro butts in, playing with the one-euro coin. "Do you have an electric drill to cut through the roof? A jackhammer? Or are you planning to amaze us by turning into the Incredible Hulk?"

"No, no, Claudia's right, I saw them do it in a Bruce Willis movie once! We can get out of here and then climb the elevator shaft, up the cables, till we reach the doors to the nearest floor and open them from the inside."

Ferro sneers, and tosses the coin again. "Calm down, young man. I'm not that young any more, I'm not climbing up any cables like Spiderman."

"We don't have to climb up any cables!" Claudia insists. "The doors to the nearest floor must be very close, they must be just above here! We just have to get through the

120

ceiling, and stand on the top of the elevator. We can open the doors from the inside."

"Listen to me. Have you looked at this elevator? It's all one piece. The ceiling, or whatever the fuck they call it, is soldered to the walls. How do you think you're going to break through that ceiling? With your bare hands?"

Claudia looks him right in the eyes. "Well, it seems stupid to me not even to give it a try."

Tomas nods frantically in agreement.

"Seeing as how the emergency services are taking their time getting here," Claudia continues, "we have to help ourselves."

Ferro sighs. He puts the coin back in his pocket, where it jangles softy against the jack knife. "Let's try it, then," he snorts, not sounding very convinced.

Tomas gets up on tiptoe and stretches his hands, as far up as they will go. His fingers don't come anywhere near the white ceiling.

"Something to stand on," he murmurs. "I can't reach. I need something to stand on."

Ferro shakes his head but cooperates, bending forward a little, putting his hands together and offering them as a support for Tomas's trainers. Tomas climbs onto this improvised ladder, tries to keep his balance, sways, rises to his full height. Claudia helps him, holding him by the sides.

Tomas touches the steel above their heads. He places his palms on the smooth surface of the ceiling and starts to push.

"Come on," Ferro pants, beneath him. "Fucking hell. Come on, I'm not twenty any more, fucking hell. I can't hold you all day."

Tomas ignores him. He's concentrating, moving his hands over the steel like a spider.

He presses, lets go, assesses the possibilities. Like a safecracker, he's looking for a spot that's more yielding than elsewhere. He strikes the ceiling with his fist, listens to the sound produced, the vibrations. He moves his hand a couple of inches and punches again.

"Move me closer to the wall," he orders, nerves stretched to breaking point.

"Oh, sure," Ferro complains. "What do you think I am, a forklift truck?" But he obeys Tomas's request. Tomas has suddenly become the focus of everything, their one hope of freedom.

They shift an inch or two towards the back of the elevator, Ferro with his hands under Tomas's shoes, Claudia gripping his sweaty sides. Tomas's naked torso sticks to the wall, his fingers worm their way into the intersection between the faces of the parallelepiped that's imprisoning them. He's looking for an imperfection in the soldering, a weak point. He doesn't find one.

The elevator is all one piece.

Impregnable.

Tomas is shaking with frustration. He launches one final rebellion against the pitiless solidity of the elevator, a violent upward push. He presses his shoes into Ferro's hands and pushes with pure force, pure rage, his teeth clenched and his eyes closed.

It's like trying to break through the roof of a car from the inside, using nothing but the strength of your arms. Inevitably, mercilessly, metal wins out over flesh.

"Shit," he hisses. "Nothing. Nothing, nothing, nothing."

"I told you," Ferro bursts out. He lets Tomas down, then collapses theatrically in the corner, next to his shirt.

For a while, there is silence, broken only by Ferro's and Tomas's laboured breathing and Claudia's angry muttering. Claudia stares up at the ceiling, unwilling to give up. That sheet of metal, that simple sheet of metal which is holding them in, imprisoning them, putting their lives on hold. A simple sheet of metal.

They check their mobiles once again. There's still no network. At last Ferro says, "This isn't a normal blackout."

Claudia glowers at him. "What do you mean?"

"It's lasted too long. Plus the alarm that doesn't make any noise, the mobiles we can't use. Come on, let's face facts. We're in the middle of an alien invasion here."

Claudia sniggers. "Of course. Why not?"

"Or an attack by Islamic extremists. Something more sophisticated than flying planes into buildings, something like an electromagnetic bomb. An electromagnetic bomb would explain the blackout, the silent alarm, the mobiles that don't work."

"It doesn't seem very likely to me," Tomas whispers, with a shudder.

Ferro fishes the coin out of his pocket again, turns it over between his fingertips, and looks at it closely. "To be honest, I'm torn between the Islamic extremist idea and the alien invasion idea. Each one, if we think about it, has points in its favour and points against."

"Enough," Claudia protests. "There's no point scaring each other."

Ferro ignores her. "Let's take the Islamic extremist idea, then. Let's suppose the attack has two distinct phases. First

123

phase, the electromagnetic bomb. At three minutes past five, it paralyses the whole city, or the whole of Italy, or the whole of the Western world, we have no way of knowing. The elevator stops, our mobiles become useless pieces of plastic and iron, the alarm is completely silent, right? OK. The first phase of the attack is followed by a second, the biological bomb. Out there, kids, everyone's dead. No one's heard us calling out, not even the old cat woman, not even the couple from Woodstock, for the simple reason that they were all writhing about on the floor and clutching their throats, unable to use either their mobiles or their landlines. We've been saved because we're stuck in here, but if we get out we'll die in a few minutes. This seems to me quite a plausible theory."

"Enough," Claudia says, curling up in a ball. "That's complete rubbish, and I've had enough. We're nervous enough already without having to make up ridiculous theories."

Again, Ferro ignores her. "Actually, I plump for the alien invasion idea. Do you want to know why? Because of the statistical anomaly. I can't really explain it in any other way. The absurd coincidence of the three of us simultaneously waiting for an elevator downstairs, with the second elevator suddenly out of order, that's something that can't be ascribed to an electromagnetic bomb or a biological attack. The aliens might have used a telepathic wave to gather the earth's population together in small groups. And now they're eating them at their leisure, in their apartments, on the streets, while we're here. In the elevator. Protected."

"ENOUGH," Claudia says again. "It's all rubbish. Complete rubbish. That's enough."

"Who can say, darling? The Apocalypse has arrived, and we're wasting time playing heads or tails." Again he looks at Claudia's thighs, and this time his gaze is obscene beyond words. Then he strokes the one-euro coin between his index and middle fingers, and turns to look at Tomas. "Well, young man, shall we play? Heads or tails?"

"I don't feel like it any more."

Ferro shrugs. "It's up to you."

Tomas is staring up at the ceiling, searching for a structural defect, a weak point, as if hoping to smash through it with the force of his mind. He has felt the steel beneath his fingers, solid and impregnable, a slab of volcanic rock. Immovable, all one piece with the walls.

He wonders what would happen if he kept hitting the same spot, over and over, first one fist then the other, until he made his hands bleed. *Would the steel give way?* he wonders.

He stops thinking, stops breathing. The little air he's breathed in is like liquid fire in his poor lungs.

You could go mad like this. The situation is unbearable.

You could go mad, mad, mad.

He needs to recover his strength, he's waiting to recover his strength. Once he's recovered his strength, he'll go back between the doors and drink in the blessed air from the elevator shaft. Once he's recovered his strength. When the heat, the thirst and the claustrophobia stop making him feel so drained.

For almost half an hour no one says a word. They are each buried in their own personal form of waiting. The only sound is the rhythmic, obsessive tinkle of the coin, which Ferro has started tossing in the air again.

125

6:45 p.m.

Claudia is huddled in her territory in the middle, sitting uncomfortably with her head between her knees.

If he doesn't stop looking at my legs, I'll smash his face.

If he doesn't stop playing with that fucking coin, I'll smash his face.

If he doesn't shut up with those little horror stories of his, I'll smash his face.

What the fuck are they doing outside? Is it possible that no one's noticed a thing?

I can't stand the stink of their sweat any more. I can't stand them being so close. Having to brush against them every time I move.

I don't trust that pig with the sideburns. I don't trust him at all. The boy seems harmless enough, but I don't trust the pig at all.

I'd like a cigarette. I'll smoke three packets as soon as I get home. I'll write to Bea with three cigarettes in my mouth. I swear. Three. Then I'll quit smoking; I managed it once before, I can do it again.

But not now.

Now I have every right to smoke three packets in a row. I must still have a few in the apartment somewhere, at the back of a drawer. The tobacconists' shops are closed, it's Sunday, it's August Bank Holiday, it's like a desert outside, nothing but lowered shutters, pavements baked by the sun, boiling tar, no shops, no people.

I must still have a few packets, at the back of a drawer somewhere.

Fuck. I wish I could stretch my legs.

Fuck. Fuck.

Claudia is huddled in her territory. Her face between her knees.

6:49 p.m.

Tomas is between the doors again, holding them open with his legs and back. He is still staring up at the untouchable ceiling.

Let me get out of here in time. That's all I ask.

The train leaves in an hour and ten minutes. If we get out now I can run to the apartment, grab my bag, and dash to the station on the Vespa.

But what if we get out and it's too late?

I have to consider the possibility that I'll miss the train. I have to consider the possibility.

I'll have to phone Francesca and tell her.

She'll understand. For sure. Nothing will happen. If the worst comes to the worst, we'll take the next train. Whatever happens. We'll take the next train. Or the one after that. It doesn't change anything. Nothing will happen.

I'm hot and cold. I have a fever. I must have a fever. I'm ill. I'm burning. And I'm cold.

Water. I could really do with some water.

If only I'd got home five minutes earlier. Or a minute earlier. Or a minute later.

If only I hadn't opened the main door to the girl with green hair. Stupid girl. I could have arrived a minute earlier. Or a minute later. Stupid girl with her weasel face and her tiny mouth and those big eyes like something out of a Japanese cartoon.

Stupid girl.

I'm thirsty.

Tomas is small and thin between the doors.

The doors seem to be crushing him like a vice.

6:53 p.m.

Ferro stares at the coin as it leaves his fingers, flies through the green air, looking as round and beautiful as the sun, and falls back into his palm. Heads. Again.

He smiles.

Even he doesn't believe in those stories of Islamic extremists and alien invasions. Not all the way, anyway.

Because if he really believed in them, if he really knew that there was nothing outside the elevator shaft any more, nothing but mountains of corpses exterminated in a biological attack, or aliens dragging human beings screaming from their cellars and sucking out their marrow as if they were lobsters, well, if he knew that all these deadly scenarios were real, he wouldn't hesitate, wouldn't feel any remorse. With no need to appear respectable any more, he would put the coin back in his pocket, take out the jack knife, cover the foot or so separating him from Tomas in a split second and cut his throat like an animal's.

And he'd really enjoy seeing the look of disbelief on that smug little face.

Then he would tear that whore's uniform off Claudia. She had to be a whore to walk around in a uniform like that, she was just a whore who wanted to be fucked in every hole like a bitch on heat. He'd fuck her till she screamed, that whore with her green hair, he'd come in her cunt and her arse and her tiny mouth and between her little tits, the whore.

And after coming to the last drop, well, the prospect of being alone in an elevator with a girl, a knife and a corpse with its throat cut, lots of time to kill and a boundless imagination – that opened up a whole lot of interesting and creative scenarios.

But for the moment, Aldo Ferro is still in control. That forty-year-old Elvis lookalike's body is still governed by the owner of three clubs called the Pink Cadillac, the Graceland and the Memphis, idol of a loyal fan club, unfaithful husband, firm but fair parent, the Aldo Ferro who is anxious to keep prying eyes out of the apartment on the twentieth floor. Determined to get out of this elevator totally anonymous, totally clean. It's that Aldo Ferro who's still in control.

The expert who can slice off a face and nail it back on upside-down, the man who makes brilliant snuff movies in the shack in the woods, the monster in the red Darth Maul mask, is still just a little voice at the back of his head. A voice like the scream of a rusty saw, a rusty saw sinking into the bark of a sequoia in a shower of sparks.

A voice that says, "There's nothing outside, the world is dead, and now I'm going to fuck this whore."

But for the moment, the voice of the Red Mask is confined to the back of his head. While Aldo Ferro, unfaithful husband, firm but fair parent, owner of three successful clubs, tosses the coin into the emerald-green air.

Again.

And again.

Hour Three

Claudia is sitting with her head between her knees. She's trying not to exist for a while.

Maybe I'll be woken by a jolt, the jolt when the elevator starts moving and the cables and counterweights come back to life. In the meantime I'm trying to sleep, to escape the horrible green light, the air that feels like wet mud, the stink of sweat. I'm going away for a while, I'm leaving you on your own, goodbye.

When she was a child, and she spent her holidays in their house in the country, Claudia used to go hunting for lizards with her brother. He was a very good hunter: he would flatten himself in the grass, wait until it was completely silent, and after a while would get back on his feet, triumphantly holding a lizard by the tail, its short legs wiggling in the air.

He would stick the lizard in a big glass jar, the one their granddad used for keeping olives, he would screw on the lid, and then run back and flatten himself in the grass. Claudia would try to imitate him, but she was too small and slow, and the tails of those repulsive descendants of the dinosaurs would always slip through her fingers.

Her brother, on the other hand, was relentless. His hunting instincts were only satisfied when there were three lizards in the jar, the perfect number for their experiments.

At this point they would seal the jar, making sure the lid was as tight as it could be. And they would start to observe.

The three lizards would dart from one corner to another, or stick like glue to the glass and look out with their stupid, cruel little eyes. They would alternate moments of sudden frenzy with others of absolute stillness. One moment they would be flat up against the sides of the jar like those Garfields you see stuck on the insides of car windows with suction pads, the next moment they would be moving about like crazed mercury, getting their tails in a tangle, nudging each other with their triangular muzzles.

When their grandmother called them back inside the house for dinner, Claudia and her brother would reluctantly hide the jar in the woodshed. They would eat hurriedly, impatient to get back and continue with the experiment, and would run back to the woodshed to take a look at the jar, wide-eyed and grinning wickedly.

They were always hoping to see the lizards eat one another. It never happened.

Their grandfather would always come into the woodshed too soon, shake his head, tell them off, and the experiment would be brought to an abrupt halt.

It would happen eventually, Claudia and her brother told each other. Their grandfather would come into the woodshed too late, and the experiment would proceed to its conclusion, with the lizards completely crazy by now and tearing each other to pieces.

* * *

Claudia has her eyes closed and her arms around her shins. She's trying to sleep.

The only problem is that in that position, with her knees under her chin, the damned uniform has an inexorable tendency to ride up her thighs. If she doesn't want to show off her store-bought knickers to the slimy Elvis lookalike, she has to keep grabbing the hem with both hands and pulling it down.

What do I do now?

How the fuck can I sleep if I have to worry about being half naked? If I have to keep this bloody uniform stretched over my legs?

She sighs. She has a fierce hatred for the Pig from the bar, but her hatred is just as strong for the pig who is breathing heavily a couple of inches away from her.

Forget about sleep, there's no way out. "We're trapped," her nerves cry out. Trapped like those lizards.

Like the little girl who scratched at the bricks.

Do you remember the little girl who scratched at the bricks?

Will you be reduced to that? Scratching at the bricks with your nails?

Will you be reduced to that? Like the little girl?

A shudder runs down her spine. She tries to think about something else. Bea. Something that reminds her of Bea. One of Bea's favourite films.

Bea loves Woody Allen, especially his films with Diane Keaton. Bea thinks Mia Farrow is just a crazy neurotic.

Claudia thinks about one of Bea's favourite films, *Manhattan Murder Mystery.*

That scene with Woody Allen and Diane Keaton in the elevator that's come to a halt between two floors, and he has an attack of claustrophobia and tries to convince himself that he's in an open space, moaning something like, "I'm a stallion and I'm running free through the meadows." Bea always laughed like a loon at that scene, laughed so hard she almost grunted like a pig.

Claudia tries to do what Woody Allen did, to imagine herself in some pleasant scenario. Some wide open space. She tries to visualize in detail the first time she met Bea. The big square, the clean air, the sky, being able to stretch her legs. Being able to move without brushing against sweaty bodies, or walls of steel. Without uniforms that ride up her thighs every time she moves.

She visualizes every detail, the smells, the lights.

The only problem, as she realizes immediately, is that if she starts on that virtual reality scenario, she can't stop it halfway. The scenario goes all the way to the end.

All the way to the little girl who scratched at the bricks.

(Will you be reduced to that, like the little girl? Scratching at the bricks with your nails?)

She grits her teeth. She's entered a mental loop she can't get out of, a vicious circle which always, inevitably, leads to the little girl. And so she tries to get out of the vicious circle with a sudden jolt inside her head, like a metal cable snapping.

She gives up on the idea of imagining herself in a wide open space, and goes back to her original idea. She tries to sleep, to escape from the elevator in her dreams at least.

She changes position a couple of times. She puts her left temple against her left knee, her right temple against her right knee, her cheeks between her knees.

"Fuck," she whispers inaudibly.

She can't do it, she can't sleep and keep the uniform pulled down at the same time. Either she resigns herself to being half naked or she gives up on the idea of sleep, because there's really no room to stretch her legs.

So she simply shuts her eyes and pretends to sleep, floating in the universe of colours behind her closed eyelids.

And she thinks again about the little girl who scratched at the bricks.

Interlude: The Little Girl Who Scratched at the Bricks

The sun was shining the first time Claudia and Bea met, but it was a deceptive sun. The biting cold still snuck its way down people's backs. Although it was autumn, it had felt like winter for some time now.

The minibus with the extras had arrived at the location in the Piazza Santo Stefano just after lunchtime. Claudia had got off in a cheerful mood. She was wearing her huge Seventies-style sunglasses, her hippy scarf, the retro jacket she'd bought in Piazzola, and her red jeans with the ripped edges. At that time, she and Ricky were extras in every film they could get into. A hundred thousand lire for an afternoon spent pretending to chat in the background of a scene. It helped to pay the rent on the apartment, and it was a pretty easy way to make a hundred thousand lire.

In March, they had walked up and down the stairs in a disco, for a film about the life of a famous cartoonist. In May, they had pretended to drink beer at the bar of a pub, in a confused and pretentious little film set among students. In June, they had repeated *peas and carrots* for a dozen takes, two out of a whole crowd of extras in a wedding reception scene.

On that freezing autumn afternoon, they simply had to be two of the spectators at a Grand Prix race in the Thirties. A hundred thousand lire for screaming and applauding as the cars roared past, an easy way to pay part of the rent for that apartment in the Via Fondazza which Claudia and Ricky shared with three rather dubious characters.

As they queued for make-up and costumes, she laughed and joked, unaware that one day she'd be moving to a twenty-storey tower block, or that sometime after that she'd be stuck in an elevator between the eleventh and twelfth floors. Standing there on the cobbles of the Piazza Santo Stefano, she couldn't have predicted any of these things.

As they were queuing for make-up and costumes, Ricky screamed "There he is!" in a voice strangled with emotion. Claudia pretended to take his pulse. "Don't die on me here," she said with a laugh.

The male star of the film had appeared in the middle of the square, already in his driver's costume, to discuss the scene with the director. Ricky was devouring him with his eyes, from a distance. He had done everything he could to be in this film and maybe get a chance to meet that actor with the aristocratic profile. "As long as I can be in the bottom corner of the screen in a scene he's in," he had said dreamily to Claudia when they were on the minibus.

Ricky was Claudia's flatmate, and her best friend. The first person she had met when she arrived in Bologna, the one refuge in that den of psychopathic students in the Via Fondazza. They had provided a crutch for each other many, many times, in those first years filled with exams and difficult love affairs. Ricky tended to fall in love with pseudo artists who inevitably turned out to be incurable bastards, while Claudia was always getting things out of proportion, always falling madly, desperately in love after a kiss, a single, usually drink-fuelled kiss at a party.

There had been one particular night when Claudia had felt as if she were one step away from the abyss. Devastated, emptied of tears, humiliated to the bone. Ricky had consoled her for hours, then had looked at her from the foot of the bed, looked right at her with a serious expression on his face, and had come out with the most absurd statement, something like, "Listen, I know you feel useless and violated right now, but if it makes you feel any better, if you ever want to give your life a meaning by becoming a mother, don't worry, I'd be proud to donate my sperm." And he had followed this absurd statement with a very deep, solemn silence.

Claudia had stared at him, puffy-eyed and incredulous, for a few moments, and then had begun to laugh uncontrollably, repeating over and over, "I'll be proud to donate my sperm! Oh, no! Where did that come from? Where did that come from?"

And in a way, it was thanks to Ricky and that crazy remark by a fervent *Will and Grace* fan that even that storm had passed.

They were together again that afternoon, queuing as usual for make-up and costumes. Claudia left the queue with a brown coat, a pair of cardboard shoes, and a little hat over an absurd Princess Leia-style hairdo; Ricky with a waistcoat, a fake moustache and a felt hat. For a while they avoided looking at each other, afraid of bursting into laughter.

There were bales of hay set up in a row just in front of the seven churches, to mark the limits of the racetrack. The extras were lined up behind these bales of hay, ready to applaud as the cars went past. They shot the scene, and the extras screamed and clapped their hands. Then they shot it again, and again, and then there was a problem with the sun and the lights, and the shooting stopped for half an hour. Claudia lit a cigarette and started complaining about the cold, because the cold air was getting in under the coat and her thighs were like two blocks of ice. And Ricky smiled broadly and said, "Leave it to me." He opened his shoulder bag and threw her a pair of legwarmers. "Put these on," he said. "The bales of hay are covering you from the waist down, no one will see them." Claudia put one hand over the other on her chest, bowed her head and fluttered her eyelids exaggeratedly, as if to say, "My hero, how can I ever thank you?"

So, while the crew was solving the problem of the lights, the story of the girl with the legwarmers under her coat did the rounds of the Piazza Santo Stefano. She responded with good humour to the jokes and comments, flashing her legwarmer-clad thighs with feigned seductiveness. And then Ricky saw Bea, who was being made up at that moment.

"Wait," he said to Claudia. "I'm going to say hello to that girl. We met on the set of that crappy film about the psychopathic innkeeper." Claudia held her nose in disgust, at the memory of that film about the psychopathic innkeeper.

Ricky ran happily over to Bea. She recognized him immediately, kissed him on the cheeks, and made a joke about his fake moustache.

Bea had a small part in this film about Grand Prix racers. She was the main character's dull, boring wife, soon to be shunted aside in favour of a mysterious and beautiful heiress who loved cars.

Claudia watched them from a distance, munching a bar

of hazelnut cream chocolate for a bit of energy. Bea could easily have entered the Miss Ireland contest, she thought. Red hair. Green eyes. Freckles.

She watched Miss Ireland from a distance, lost in thought, and then, suddenly, Ricky brought her over, crying, "Claudia, this is Bea!"

Claudia fluttered her eyelashes a couple of times, wiping her chocolate-stained hands on her costume. She introduced herself to the potential Miss Ireland, and the potential Miss Ireland warbled, "The girl with the legwarmers!" and Ricky laughed, with that little laugh of his that sounded like a goose with a cold.

That was how they met, in the middle of a square suffused with an ice-cold sun, Bea all done up as a dull and boring wife and Claudia with legwarmers under her coat and a bar of hazelnut cream chocolate in her hand, in the shadow of the seven churches of the Piazza Santo Stefano.

The shooting finished at sunset. Friendships had formed that afternoon, and it would have been a pity for them to disappear the way the handsome actor playing the main character had disappeared after the last take.

Claudia and Ricky dragged Bea and a small group of extras and costume people to an old tavern, where they ate and drank and laughed, then a few went home but a small group got back in their cars, eager to continue the evening one way or another. They set off for Primo Maggio, just outside the city, where there was apparently a pub which offered free card readings. And after the free card reading, as it was now the middle of the night, the group thinned out even more.

There were still six of them who didn't want to go home to sleep, six people in one car. Claudia, Ricky, Bea, two extras who looked like Laurel and Hardy, one a fat guy with a moustache, the other thin and dumb-looking, and another man who had been with them all evening and hadn't said a word. Whether he was an extra, a make-up man, or just a sad passer-by who'd tagged along because he thought they could show him a good time, no one knew. Some things don't matter on evenings like that.

They had been standing outside the pub for a while, chatting and considering various possible destinations, discos, pubs, when Bea clicked her fingers.

"I'll show you the haunted house!" she cried. "I'll show you the haunted house!"

The idea was greeted with unprecedented enthusiasm. No one wanted any details. They were all too drunk to ask questions. All six got back in Bea's car, Claudia on Ricky's lap in the back seat next to Laurel and Hardy, and the silent stranger in the front passenger seat.

Bea drove out of the industrial district, past a small suburban station, and turned onto a winding country road. They drove for a couple of miles between fields, until, suddenly, they found themselves in no man's land.

They had turned a bend and all at once there were no more yellow lights, only a wall of shadow and a thin mist that obscured the road.

"Let me show you something incredible," Bea said, wild-eyed. They continued for about a hundred yards in the cream-coloured mist, and after another bend the car was back in the world, with yellow lights, clear air, the white line on the road.

142

She made a sudden U-turn, the rear wheels screeching on the edge of a field, and they plunged back into the darkness and mist.

"Guess where the haunted house is," she said with a derisive smile.

Claudia and Ricky rapidly exchanged glances, and he whispered in her ear, "She's pretty, but crazy as a loon!" and she nodded, agreeing about both points. Then Bea pulled up, close to a wall in which there was a huge gate.

"Here it is!" she said, cleverly lowering her voice. She pointed the headlights at the gate.

Beyond the gate, surrounded by trees and shrouded in mist, stood an abandoned mansion.

They got out of the car to look at the mansion, sticking their heads through the bars of the gate. As Bea started speaking, the mist caused little drops to form under Claudia's jacket.

"This is the haunted house," Bea whispered. "It was built on the ruins of an earlier mansion. Destroyed in a fire."

Claudia laughed. "I've heard that one before. Sam Raimi, wasn't it?"

But Bea ignored her. "What happened was this. One night, the owner of the original mansion discovered his wife and his brother in the hayloft, in a situation that left no room for doubt, if you know what I mean. They didn't see or hear him. He went and fetched a rifle, went back to the hayloft, and shot his brother between the legs. Then, while his wife was screaming, bathed in her lover's blood, he shot her between the legs too. He dragged them both into the mansion, bleeding and half dead, and tied them together on the floor of the drawing room, face to face, their wounds touching. Then he went upstairs, locked the room where his children were sleeping, and set fire to the mansion. Finally, he went back down to the drawing room, poured himself a drink and waited to die."

Claudia was about to make another joke, but it died in her throat. There was something magnetic about that house. Something as hypnotic and enticing as the eyes of a cobra.

She looked through the bars of the gate again.

There was a bunch of roses at the foot of the gate. A bunch of roses, just flung there among the weeds.

And the moonlight, filtering through the mist, etched strange shadows on the front door of the house. Not just the shadows of trees.

They seemed to form a large black cross.

Bea continued her story, like a guide on a horror tour. "The second mansion was built on the ashes of the previous one by a rich landowner. He and his wife came to live here at the turn of the century. It was in this house that the little girl was born."

She paused for effect. Waiting for someone – Ricky, as it turned out – to ask, "What little girl?"

"The little girl who could see the future," she replied, slyly. She looked at the members of her audience in turn: Claudia, Ricky, Laurel and Hardy, the unknown man. "Who could see things a few days before they happened. Who could recite poetry in Greek and Latin, even though she'd never learned Greek or Latin. Who swore over and over again that there was a little boy under her bed, and that she'd talked to him, and become friends with him."

Claudia laughed again. "Nicole Kidman, right? *The Others*." No one else laughed. The idea of laughing, the very concept of laughing, seemed totally out of place here, outside that house.

Bea continued her story, as precise and polished as a tour guide. "Now, as you can imagine, for a God-fearing, superstitious family at the turn of the century, anything supernatural had to be the work of the devil. And so the little girl's father walled her up alive. Walled her up in her own room."

"Fuck!" one of the Laurel and Hardy duo cried.

Bea pointed to a window, the one that seemed to glow the brightest in the moonlight. "That was the little girl's room," she said. "Her father boarded up the window to stop her jumping out, but the boards have long gone. She died there, behind the wall, just a few inches from her parents. But inside the house, you can still hear her crying or begging for help. Some people swear they've seen her playing with a ball in the dark corridors. Shall we go in?"

And she looked them all in the eyes, to see their reactions to this unexpected proposition.

Claudia felt her knees turn to milk, but she didn't let it show. Pretending to be practical, she examined the gate and the wall around the mansion.

"The wall's too high," she observed. "How do we get in, by flying?"

Ricky and the others agreed, visibly relived.

Bea laughed. "You can't get in through the main entrance, in fact. But there's a waste pipe in the brickwork. There, do you see? That round opening in the wall? It

145

hasn't rained for two weeks, so the pipe should be dry. Well? Who's with me?"

Ricky looked at her wide-eyed. "We're supposed to get inside the house through that?"

"It's only about thirty yards. We creep into the pipe, and come out in the cellar. From there, there's a staircase leading to the other floors. You just have to be careful because the wood is half rotten. I have a torch in the car. Shall we go?"

"The *cellar*?" one of the Laurel and Hardy duo gasped.

"A wooden staircase that's *rotten*?" Ricky said.

The silent man said nothing as usual.

Bea shook her head. "Huh! I knew you'd all be scared shitless in the end." She looked straight at Claudia. "You'll come, though, won't you?"

Claudia heard a voice coming out of her mouth, a voice that sounded like her own voice, replying automatically, "Of course I will."

"Be careful," Ricky whispered behind her. Claudia answered with a reassuring gesture, and followed Bea and the beam of the torch into the pipe.

She had to bend forward until she was almost on all fours in order to enter that cylinder in the brickwork. By the time they'd gone a few yards, the world outside had been swallowed by the mist.

Ricky, Laurel and Hardy, the silent man, the car – they were all gone, and there was nothing left but the tread of their feet on the floor of the tunnel and the smell of stagnant water, rotted leaves and decomposing rodents that assaulted her nostrils.

"Scared?" Bea asked, to provoke her.

"I'm not scared of anything," she replied, falling into the role of the dumb teenage boy in horror movies. The one who goes into the abandoned house to impress the girl and show her how brave he is, and two minutes later is suddenly decapitated by a cackling witch.

They crept through the tunnel for an entire geological era, until finally Bea whispered, "Here we are," and shone her torch on the walls of the cellar.

A few years earlier, Claudia had gone to the premiere of *The Blair Witch Project*. She'd gone with Ricky, and they'd promised to cover each other's eyes during the scary bits.

In fact, for most of the film they didn't need to do that. They munched their jumbo-sized popcorn, their feet up on the backs of the row in front, laughing out loud at certain moments that they found unintentionally funny. They were quite bored with all that subjective camerawork as the kids wandered in the woods. Until, in the last five minutes, the survivors entered the haunted house, and for the first time in the film Claudia found herself shuddering a little.

She really hadn't been scared by the woods, the open spaces, the darkness between the branches. She hadn't felt even slightly in sympathy with the anxieties of the characters lost in the forest. But, inevitably, what got to her was the predictable archetype of the cursed house. The place that should, by definition, be welcoming and friendly, the maternal womb, the place supposed to protect you from the outside world, which suddenly, without mercy, kills you.

And so, without letting Ricky notice, she watched the last

five minutes of the film through half-closed eyes, so that she shared only partly the terror of the female character, who continued right to the end filming the stone steps, the abandoned rooms, the graffiti on the peeling walls. Her friend with his face turned to the wall, in the last scene, the final darkness.

The video camera on the cold floor.

Now, as she entered a *real* haunted house, Claudia adopted the same means to protect herself from the terror she felt. She narrowed her eyes to a crack, through which she saw only Bea's back and the beam of light from the torch, and made an effort not to see anything she was passing. She did this in the cellar, on the wooden stairs with their creaking steps, and then in the drawing room. Especially in the drawing room.

Out of the corner of her eye, she sensed how frighteningly large the room was. Maybe it had been built on the ashes of the original drawing room, she thought. The one in which a man had sat in an armchair, near where his brother and wife lay bound and bleeding on the floor, and waited for the flames to consume him, while ignoring the screams of his children burning upstairs.

There was a different smell in this room. A mixture of cinnamon and boiling wax. The room was too big. There might be evil things, hungry things, crouching in the furthest corners, in the dark. Better not to look, better to concentrate on Bea's back and the light of the torch. Better not to look at anything at all.

Bea strode across the room. "Oh, I forgot to tell you," she said, as if it were the most natural thing in the world. "They sometimes celebrate black masses here."

Thanks, Claudia thought. *Now I feel better. A whole lot better. Thanks for setting my mind at rest.*

She didn't even have time to reply. Bea had already moved to the stone staircase. Claudia followed her up the damp, cold steps to the upper floor. They found themselves in a long, bare corridor. The beam of light moved over the worm-eaten door frames, the remains of rooms in which people had once lived, as Bea searched for a particular spot, smiling in a sinister way.

She shone the torch at the walled-up door.

"This was the little girl's room," she said, smiling triumphantly, her eyes gleaming. She moved the beam of light down, to reveal a gap in the wall, some three feet wide, as if a battering ram had gone through it.

As Claudia followed Bea through the gap, she tried to isolate her thoughts from the noise inside her head and the pounding of her heart.

OK, let's be clear about this.

I'm not scared of anything.

I'm not scared of anything.

But.

If I hear something.

Something that even vaguely resembles a child crying.

Or a ball bouncing.

I'll die here.

I'm not scared of anything.

But this.

Quite frankly.

Is a bit too much.

If a mouse scurries out.

Even just a mouse.

149

I'll be out of here at the speed of light.
And I won't stop till I get to Kansas.

The light in the room was yellowish-blue and opaque. The moon hit the peeling walls through a huge hole in the roof, piercing the veil of mist. Bea pointed to the hole with a movement of her head.

"You see? When there's a full moon, the light hits the window. From outside, it looks as if a light has come on in the room. Evocative, isn't it?"

"Fairly," Claudia agreed, as she picked her way through rubble and leaves and something else that felt strange underfoot, like soggy straw. She went to the window, and tried to see Ricky on the other side of the gate, but couldn't make out anything between the tall, dark shapes of the huge trees in the mist.

"Look," Bea called to her, shining the torch at the walled-up door.

Claudia looked for something unusual in the circle of light, but all she could see were red bricks. She looked up at Bea. "What exactly am I supposed to be looking at?"

"The marks." Pointing out a number of parallel vertical lines, just about visible on the bricks, she bared her white teeth in the moonlight in a sadistic smile. "The little girl's nails. When she was trying to get out. Trying to dig her way out with her bare hands."

Claudia looked at the marks wide-eyed.

At that desperate attempt at survival by a little girl who had scratched at the stone until she had worn her fingers to the bone. She could almost see her, alone in that room, without food, without water, her voice gone after

150

screaming for days on end, calling to her parents in vain. On her knees on the floor.

But Claudia, well, Claudia was the woman who wasn't scared of anything. And so she concealed the horror she felt and said in a firm voice, "It's now that the ghost appears, right?"

Bea gave her a dirty look. "What ghost?"

"The ghost of the little girl. Come on, I've seen tons of horror movies. The two bimbos who've gone into the haunted house find themselves face to face with the ghost of the little girl, all white, with her fingers eaten down to the bone."

Bea laughed. "You're really weird, you know."

"Wait, wait, I haven't finished. The ghost cuts the throat of one of the two bimbos, probably you, and the other one runs away. She runs all through the house, stumbles on the rotten stairs, pushes her way past skeletons and cobwebs, and finally gets to the walled-up door. At that point she turns round, gives a big scream in close-up, and the ghost kills her too."

"You know something? You're starting to scare me a little. Just a little."

"That was my intention. Shall we play a joke on the others?"

"What kind of joke?"

"We climb out along the branches of the trees like Tarzan, we get over the wall, and we come out behind them screaming like banshees. Are you up for it?"

Bea laughed. "If we do that, the fat guy will die on the spot."

"Better still. There'll be more room for us in the car."

They carried on in this vein for a while, before leaving the haunted mansion.

Anything so as not to think about those marks on the wall. Those little nails trying to make an impossible opening.

Impossible

(like breaking through steel with your hands, getting out of an elevator with nothing but the strength of your arms)

to imagine the coldness of a soul imprisoned between four walls, with no hope of escape, with her life being slowly sucked out of her, slowly, slowly, like

(being inside an elevator stuck between the eleventh and twelfth floors)

a whirlpool, and Claudia blinks, closing her eyes and opening them again, and suddenly she's no longer in the haunted mansion with a girl named Bea who she's only known for a few hours. She's back in the elevator, between four metal walls, with two men consuming her precious oxygen.

She grinds her teeth so loudly, she rouses Tomas from his torpor. He looks up for a moment, distracted by that irritating noise, then goes back into his own world.

Claudia tries to wind back the tape.

She again visualizes the wide, spacious square, the sun, the clean air, she feels good, she feels free. But the tape runs through to the end, all the way to a little girl so close to the edge between life and death she's prepared to wear her fingers to the bone on the bricks.

And then she comes out of the film. She concentrates on the metal plate showing the elevator's maximum weight and capacity, and on her knees which are bent in an unnatural position and screaming in agony, and on the hem of her uniform.

Anything to chase away the idea of herself kneeling in front of the elevator doors. Crazed with fear, scratching at the solid concrete of the elevator shaft.

Hour Four

"Biscuits?" Ferro mutters, his voice low and gurgling, like pebbles churning in the drum of a washing machine.

Claudia coughs. "That's all I have." She's divided her ration of biscuits into three.

Ferro grinds his teeth loudly. "If that's all there is," he says, "then let's enjoy this lovely delicacy."

His face is as black as thunder. He looks feverishly at Claudia, then at Tomas, then at the walls of the elevator. Moving his head jerkily, like the Terminator, he clutches at his biscuit like a spider grabbing a fly and feels its texture with his fingers.

"It's almost melted," he complains. "It's half melted. Fuck."

Claudia shrugs. "Heat" is all she says. She's economizing on words. Her mouth is so dry it feels like cardboard. Talking hurts, and breathing is an agony.

Ferro breaks the biscuit in two, puts half in his mouth, and chews slowly, staring blankly into the green light. Then he forgets all about rationing the food and stuffs everything in his mouth. He chomps on it, and swallows it down quickly. His hands are smeared and sticky.

Claudia coughs again. "Tomas? I have biscuits. Do you want some?"

155

Tomas doesn't answer. He's crouching at the back of the elevator, and hasn't said a word for twenty minutes. His eyes are closed as if he's asleep. Every now and again, his body is shaken by powerful, convulsive shudders.

"Tomas?" Claudia says again. She reaches out her hand to touch his shoulder, and he recoils, moaning, "I don't want anything. I really don't want anything."

"Let him die of starvation," Ferro barks. "If he doesn't want to eat, let him die of starvation."

Claudia prefers to ignore him, otherwise she'd have to insult him. She's dying to smoke a cigarette, have a drink, stretch her legs. She chews slowly.

It'll give you a bit of energy, but it'll make your thirst worse, you know that, don't you?

It's good to get a bit of energy, because the heat and the waiting and being unable to move are making you as dry as a run-down battery, but in a while the thirst will start to drive you crazy. You don't yet know what it means to be thirsty, girl. You really will end up drinking your own urine and being grateful for it, you know that, don't you?

She puts the biscuit Tomas refused back in her bag; best to keep it for when things get even worse, and to her surprise touches something at the bottom. Something small and smooth and forgotten.

Startled, she glances over at Ferro, but Ferro isn't looking at her. He's eating in silence, with his eyes down, like a lion in the savannah. He's not paying any attention to her.

So Claudia opens the Peruvian bag, just enough so that she can look inside. What she finds is a packet of coffee-filled chocolates.

A packet she didn't remember having in her bag.

A light goes on in her head. *The Subsonica concert!* The Subsonica concert at the beginning of the summer, the club full to bursting, the heat enough to drive you crazy. Sweaty bodies rubbing up against each other. And that thirst she felt halfway through the concert as she was singing all the choruses at the top of her voice, a thirst brought on by the furnace-like heat in that tangle of bodies beneath the stage. Just a touch, of course, compared with *real* thirst, the kind she's feeling now after being stuck in this elevator for three and a quarter hours, but it seemed unbearable at the time.

The bar was on the other side of the club, and reaching it meant abandoning the place she'd managed somehow to grab for herself, pushing through the crowd, elbowing her way to the bar, then going all the way back again, this time with a beer in her hand, and trying to get her place back, the whole undertaking slowed down by the fact that she was carrying a plastic cup full to the brim. Twenty minutes of the concert wasted. At least.

So she had an idea. She stuffed one coffee-filled chocolate after another into her mouth, sucking the coffee out of its chocolate casing like a bee. It was liquid, after all.

A palliative it may have been, but it helped her to get to the end of the concert and a well-deserved final beer without being reduced to sucking her own sweat, or begging for a drop of water from one of her neighbours against the crush barrier.

Light years now from that carefree moment, Claudia has one hand stuffed inside the Peruvian bag. Making sure the others aren't watching her, she feels the packet to check its exact contents.

Four remaining chocolates. Four.

Half melted from the heat, to judge from the shape. *Incredible, though,* she thinks, *that they've survived this inferno.*

Claudia squeezes the open end of the packet between two fingers and pops one of the chocolates out, half melted but still full of precious liquid. Patiently, she unwraps it, without taking it out of the bag. The chocolate is soft and sticky.

Ferro isn't looking. Now's the moment.

Quick as a flash, she lifts the chocolate to her mouth, bites into it, and closes her eyes. She's in heaven.

Drops of coffee.

Liquid.

Cascading into her parched mouth.

The liquid reaches every spot on her rough palate, her cement tongue, her leathery cheeks. Resuscitating and redeeming every corner it touches.

For Claudia, it's the best moment she's had since she got in the elevator.

When she's drunk every last drop of coffee, Claudia gulps down the half-melted chocolate. There are three other chocolates in the packet, all laden with liquid, three vital resources. They have to stay at the bottom of the bag, well hidden. They're hers and hers alone.

Now that she's got some of her energy back, Claudia is able to face the situation. She looks at Tomas, rolled up like a bundle against the doors.

"Tomas?" she murmurs gently, able to articulate clearly again. "Tomas? Are you OK?"

"No," Tomas groans, without turning to look at her. "I'm not OK. I'm not OK at all." He coughs. "I'm thirsty. I'm dying of thirst. I missed my train, the train has already left and I'm still in this fucking elevator. I absolutely have to make a phone call, and this fucking mobile keeps telling me there's no network. I think I have a fever. I'm not OK. I'm not OK at all."

"Why not have a good cry, then, kid?" Ferro says, provoking him, his eyes coloured by a web of thin red veins. "Why not stamp your little feet on the ground? Maybe your fairy godmother will get you out of here. What do you say, kid? Stamp your feet on the ground, go on. Give us a laugh. Stamp your feet on the ground."

"That's enough," Claudia says angrily.

"Like fuck it is," Ferro snarls, getting to his feet.

Claudia tenses. She flattens herself against the wall.

Oh, God. Oh, God, he's gone crazy. Look at his eyes. He's gone crazy.

Seeing the frightened look on her face, Ferro gives a phlegm-laden laugh. He raises his hands. "Hey, kid, calm down. I'm not going to rape you. There wouldn't even be room." He laughs nervously at his own joke. "But fuck it, I really need a cigarette. If I don't smoke I turn nasty, and when that happens I'm not responsible for my own actions. You don't want to see Aldo Ferro turn nasty, do you?"

"There's no air in here," Claudia whispers, glancing at Tomas out of the corner of her eye, as if appealing to him for help. She doesn't get any. Tomas isn't there, he's somewhere else. "I'd like to smoke too, but there's no air in here at all."

"I know, kid, I know, I breathe too, what do you think,

I have gills? So I'll be good, and keep away from the no-smoking area. I'll have my smoke outside. You two hold the doors open for me." He reaches out his leg and touches Tomas with the tip of his boot. "Hey, kid, did you hear me? I have to go for a smoke outside. Be good, the two of you, and hold the doors open for me. If not I'll turn nasty."

Mechanically, Claudia stands up, gritting her teeth. Her stiff knees are screaming with pain.

For a moment there, she was scared, *really* scared.

Claudia isn't someone who scares easily, but when she looked in Ferro's eyes she was really scared. When she looked into those two dark wells, two dark wells with nothing behind them.

At that moment she had a really bad feeling. She was no longer in an elevator with two strangers, a teenage boy, harmless and trustworthy, and a man who's unpleasant but no more dangerous than the bastard who hits your car and then stands in the middle of the road, screaming that he's in the right and refusing to sign any forms. When she saw those two dark wells, when she heard that hollow voice snarling, she felt as if she was somewhere where the rules didn't apply, a limbo in which anything could happen. Her only ally was a lot younger and infinitely weaker than the enemy. She was scared. And she obeyed.

Tomas takes a while to emerge from his sad universe, a universe full of trains running along tracks, and girls waiting anxiously at stations, and unusable telephones. He gets to his feet, dripping sweat, and shuffles to the wall on the other side from Claudia, brushing against Ferro's sweaty skin and the steel surfaces.

They open the doors.

Claudia holds the left one open, Tomas the right.

Ferro coughs. "Thanks, kids. If you're good, Uncle Aldo will be generous with the pocket money."

He stands on the runner and puts his head out into the elevator shaft. He leans out into the three inches at his disposal and searches in his pocket for the packet of cigarettes and the lighter. In a meticulous ritual, he slides a cigarette out of the packet, lights it, inhales voluptuously, and lets the smoke drift out into the elevator shaft.

Claudia and Tomas are forced to flatten themselves against the walls, to hold themselves as far as possible inside the elevator and stretch their arms to maintain their grip on the door. It's an uncomfortable, unnatural position. They stand firm with their feet on the bubbled rubber, like two servants making room for their master.

Claudia grits her teeth. The pressure exerted by these strangely springy doors is incredible, the obstinacy with which they try to get back together. It's not springs they seem to have, she thinks, so much as magnets. These doors are *magnetic.*

Tomas is making a similar effort on the other side, a vacant look in his eyes, his arm muscles taut. In between them the Elvis lookalike is smoking calmly, bare-chested, sending filigreed smoke rings into the elevator shaft. He drops the ash down eleven floors as if he were on the balcony of his apartment. Claudia and Tomas stand there like his fans, their arms outstretched like Mister Fantastic.

As if we weren't exhausted enough by the heat, the thirst, the immobility, the claustrophobia, Claudia thinks angrily, *oh no, we also have to struggle with doors that slip from under our fingers, just so this sweaty bastard can smoke in peace.*

She hates him. She could bear all this torture, the waiting, the immobility, if her only companion in misfortune were Tomas.

But this horrible man, with his rank smell of sweat, with his tufts of hair on the back and shoulders, with all the loathing he keeps hidden behind a facade of falsely bohemian respectability, all this just makes her want to bite and scratch. The grating sensation at the back of her neck pulsates as if it wanted to grow, as if it wanted to spread through her bones.

She looks at Tomas, hanging on to the door to the right of the monster. She looks at Tomas, and sees only a sack of empty flesh. She sees the muscles tensing, the feet planted on the rubber floor, but his mind and his eyes are far away from this coffin of green light and stainless steel. His mind is on a railway track somewhere, pursuing a train, and the train is on its way towards a waiting girl who's convinced there's a person on that train who has come to take her away like the knight in a fairy tale. A person who has come to save her life. The same person who's now standing bare-chested in an elevator, bent forward, close to the walls, with his hands clinging to the edge of a door, a sheet of metal against which his poor tortured muscles are fighting a losing battle.

And all at once, while Ferro is sending the umpteenth elaborate smoke ring into the elevator shaft, Tomas's mind detaches itself a little too much from his body. His sweaty fingers slip on the steel, his shoes slide backwards, his body loses balance, and his arms give way.

By the time Tomas's eyes come back to life it's too late. The steel door has already shot along the runner like the jaw of a trap.

162

Ferro moves his head back just in time, but the door smashes into his right foot.

Ferro lets out a scream. He throws his cigarette in the air and leaps back, his body twisted in a way that's both dramatic and comic.

Claudia lets go of the door, which joins its twin with a metallic clang. The cigarette describes an arc in the green air and falls to the floor beneath the control panel.

"I'm sorry, I'm sorry," Tomas stammers, as if he's just landed from a distant world to take responsibility for his own body. "I didn't do it on purpose, I swear, I didn't do it on purpose."

Ferro collapses at the back of the elevator, cursing and holding his foot. "Fucking idiot!" he barks. "Fucking idiot! You did it on purpose, you fucking idiot, you fucking fairy, you did it on purpose, fuck you, fuck you!" He takes off the boot, touches his foot, and lets out another scream. His ankle is too painful to touch.

In a while it'll be swollen like a puffer fish. Fuck.

How am I going to drive my car when we get out of here? How am I going to get back to the shack if I can't use this foot?

Shit.

Shit.

Shit.

"You broke my foot!" he snarls. "You broke it, you dickhead, you fucking idiot!"

He sticks his hand in the pocket where the knife is, his eyes brimming with hate. Then he feels a strong stab of pain in his ankle and grits his teeth.

"I'm sorry," Tomas moans. "I'm sorry. I didn't do it on purpose. The door was heavy. My fingers were sweaty."

163

"You can't have broken your foot," Claudia says. "You've just had a knock. It'll get a bit swollen, that's all."

"That's right, go on, defend him, defend him, I'm crippled here and you're defending him, great. Why don't you give him a blowjob while you're about it? At least I'll have something interesting to look at. Oh fuck, fuck, it fucking hurts." He keeps looking at his foot as if he wanted to amputate it. "You'll pay for this, you fairy, you fucking idiot."

(His fingers tighten on the knife. The dam gives way. The walls collapse. The world explodes. There are scarlet spots behind his eyelids.)

Claudia stubs out the still lighted cigarette beneath her foot. The grating sensation continues to burrow down into her spine.

She's about to speak, but then she feels something. Something unexpected and wonderful.

Tomas is still whining hysterically, "It wasn't my fault, I swear, I swear, I didn't do it on purpose," but Claudia silences him.

"It moved! Did you feel it? It moved!"

Tomas and Ferro both prick up their ears at the same time. Their expressions change instantly.

"What?" Ferro mutters. "What moved?"

"The elevator! The elevator! It moved! I felt it! It moved!"

Ferro jumps up, balancing on his left foot and the heel of his right foot. He pounds on the wall, screaming, "We're in here! We're in here, you bastards! Is there anyone there? We're in here!"

He rushes forward, trying not to shift his weight onto his injured ankle. He rubs against Tomas and Claudia, raising sprays of sweat as their bodies make contact. He puts his hands on the control panel and presses the alarm button six times, yelling, "We're in here! We're in here, you bastards! We're in here!"

He presses his ear to the wall. Laboriously, pursing his lips and gritting his teeth, working from pure adrenalin, Tomas manages to get the doors open again.

He can only open them an inch or two. He looks at the wall of the elevator shaft. "It isn't moving," he moans.

Ferro silences him, frowning. He looks at Claudia, hopefully. "Did it move? Are you sure it moved?"

She waits an eternity before replying. "Maybe. I think so. I thought it did."

For a few minutes the three of them stand there, in silence, in the green light. Then Tomas gives up, and collapses to the floor beneath the control panel.

"It did move," Claudia swears, damp-eyed. "It did move."

Ferro sits down again and massages his bare foot, muttering strange, inarticulate curses between his teeth.

"It did move," Claudia moans. "It did move."

In the end, she falls silent too.

8:50 p.m.

The sand is going down in the hourglass, the spider's voice in Tomas's head croons, the sand is going down in the hourglass, how much sand is left in the hourglass, oh, look, not very much.

Shut up.

Oh, look, there's not much sand left in the hourglass, not much sand at all, think about Francesca, Francesca has already left home, Francesca is already at the station, she's counting the minutes, Francesca with her little case and her little watch and her happy little brain, turning over happily as she waits, poor Francesca.

Shut up.

Oh, there's not much left, not much at all, four minutes, think about the train stopping at the platform, and there she'll be, anxious and very beautiful, with a knot in her stomach and her heart pounding, looking for your face among all the other faces, poor disappointed kid.

Shut up. Bastard.

What will she do, poor Francesca, when the train has left again and the platform has emptied and there's no sign of you? She'll grab the phone, of course. She'll call your mobile. What will she think when she hears a recorded voice that keeps saying *The number you are calling is currently unobtainable?* What will she think of you?

She'll dial your home number, a storm raging in her chest, her eyes a lake of tears. How many times will she let it ring before she gives up?

Ten times?

Twenty times?

How many times will she let it ring?

"Hey, kid. Come here."

Tomas opens his eyes, and returns to reality. Ferro is staring at him through the green light.

He has circles round his eyes, which seem deeply

embedded in his skull. They look strange, those eyes, in the emerald light. They look *yellow*.

"Come closer, kid," Ferro whispers, as if they weren't a foot or so from each other. Tomas glances at Claudia, who is now leaning against the doors, huddled over her Peruvian bag, apparently asleep.

"I'm not going to do anything to you, kid. I just want to talk to you."

Somewhat reluctantly, Tomas leans forward.

Ferro also glances over at Claudia, then starts speaking very softly and slowly. "Let's you and me make a pact, kid. I'm a reasonable man, you know. Maybe I go a little crazy sometimes, just like everyone else, it's hot, my ankle hurts, I'm thirsty, I go a little crazy like everyone else, but then I reason things out. I'm quite capable of doing that. When you shut the door on my foot, my first reaction was to strangle you with these hands —"

"I didn't do it on purpose, it was —"

"All right, all right, let me speak. I just want to say I'm not angry with you, you didn't do it on purpose, it was an accident, of course. In a situation like this we men have to stay united; women always try to come between us, to divide us, but men have to stay united, am I right?"

Tomas nods, without understanding. Ferro gives a derisive smile, revealing his teeth.

"That's good, kid. You can see I'm a reasonable man, can't you? That I don't bear you any grudge?" He nods towards Claudia. "Not like that half-crazy woman with her green hair. Anyone can see straight away she's a ball-breaker, pretending she's so tough, fucking us around the way she did, telling us the elevator had moved, deceiving us

167

like that, the bitch, pretending she's so tough, but I bet you she's been all wet these past four hours, because women get wet when they're tense, you know? For the last four hours she's been acting so stand-offish, and in the meantime she's all wet and she keeps thinking, 'But what about these two, why don't they just take out their cocks and screw me like they're supposed to, what are they, impotent? Here I am, half naked, and they don't do what's only natural to do in a situation like this.' So you know what we should do, kid, just tell me if you don't like the idea, we should pull down our trousers, wake her up, and when she opens her eyes the first thing she sees is our cocks all fired up and ready to go, what do you say to that? Doesn't that get you excited? It gets me excited, I can tell you, so what do you say, shall we do it?"

Tomas swallows. He can feel icy fingers up and down his spine. "I have a girlfriend," he stammers.

Ferro waves his hand as if swatting a fly. "What's that got to do with anything? I'm married. You didn't believe what I told her earlier? That was a load of bullshit, that's what you do with girls, you tell them a load of bullshit, I'm married, I even have a son, but what's that got to do with anything, do you think the bitch will be offended because I have a wife and son? Look how she's dressed, don't you think a girl who dresses like that wants one thing and one thing only, and that's a man's cock? She looks so innocent with that little face of hers, but you know what I think, I think she's the kind of girl who doesn't just take it in her mouth and swallow it down to the last drop, oh, no, listen to the voice of experience, you won't find anyone more experienced than me, kid, she's one of those girls who go to work on you with their tongues and at the same time look up at you with their eyes wide open, they want to see you when you come, I know girls like that, all they think about is men's cocks, so what do you say, are you in?"

Tomas's nerves seem to be pulling in every direction. He's aware of every one of them. He can feel them stretching under his silky-thin skin.

"I don't think it'd be right," he stammers finally.

(Why the fuck are you wasting your time talking to this stupid kid? Take out the knife! Stick it in his throat! Right in his throat!)
(No. I can't. They'd find out everything. The apartment. The shack. Everything. I have to stay calm, think things through. Stay calm, think things through.)

Ferro shakes his head, sniggers, and mumbles something.

Then he goes back to massaging his foot, concentrating on his swollen ankle.

What's all that whispering? Claudia wonders half-asleep, wrapped in a cocoon of merciful semi-consciousness. *What are they talking about? Why do they have to whisper? Are they talking about me?*

Inside the cocoon, the grating sensation at the back of her neck has become a little steel ball.

The little steel ball throbs like a black sun behind her neck.

Inside the cocoon, Claudia is trying in vain to visualize Bea's face.

She concentrates, digging in the spongy recesses of her memory, coming up with vague impressions of eyes, a nose, a mouth, trying to put them together to make a face.

But the details, the details just keep slipping away.

All she can recall is a mannequin with a blank oval instead of a head. She sees herself strolling through the narrow streets of the Ghetto district with a faceless mannequin, going to the cinema with a faceless mannequin, waking up on a rainy morning beside a faceless mannequin. She can't remember her face. She's forgotten her face.

Except.

Maybe.

There!

An image emerges from the spongy fabric, there she is, Bea, there are her freckles, there's her red hair, there are her perfect teeth, there she is, Bea! A memory of that winter evening, the first snowfall of the year, Claudia and Bea entering the twenty-storey building, they're in a cheerful mood, they have wet, dripping hair, they get in the elevator

(in the elevator)

Bea is holding a bag from the video rental store containing *Love and Death* and *Annie Hall*, Claudia is holding the boxes of pizza and complaining because the boxes of pizza are burning hot and dripping oil, and they both laugh because the heat rising from the boxes is condensing on the white ceiling of the elevator

(*this* elevator)

and Bea uses her free hand to press the button, and the electric doors close

(*these* doors)

and, as always, the elevator ascends, stops at their floor, the doors open, Claudia and Bea get out of the elevator

(*this* elevator)

and as soon as they set foot on the landing Bea's features dissolve and she's once again a mannequin with an empty oval instead of a face, a mannequin holding a bag from the video rental store containing *Love and Death* and *Annie Hall*, and at this point the *real* Claudia starts to cry, the little steel ball moves into her sternum and starts to throb, and when the tears overflow from behind her eyelids and the throbbing behind her ribs is too intense, Claudia wakes up.

Cast out of a pink-and-white world, back into the emerald-coloured world.

She looks at the elevator – the same elevator where the heat caused condensation to form on the steel, the elevator where she joked with Bea – she looks at it and sees Ferro massaging his bare foot, Tomas playing desperately with his keys, and the walls, which seem very, very near.

She tries to go back inside the cocoon, but going back inside the cocoon is impossible.

So instead she latches on to a more reassuring thread of thoughts.

The Falco series of Nembo Kid, six hundred and fifty-one issues. From issue 529 the name changes to Superman Nembo Kid. From issue 575 the name changes to Superman Mondadori.

Nembo Kid Supercomics, eighty-five issues. From issue 62 the name changes to Batman Nembo Kid.

Superman Williams first series, sixteen issues.

Superman Williams second series, eleven issues.

Superseries, twenty-six issues.

Superman Cenisio . . .

She gets as far as the Superman TPs from Play Press. Then she winds back the thread and starts all over again.

Hour Five

A sound penetrates the green air, distant but clearly audible.

A sound coming from one of the apartments. A telephone ringing.

The executioner's blade.

"There it is," Tomas moans, his head between his knees.

He knows perfectly well where that call is coming from. From the station in Parma. Via the fifteenth floor.

"A tiny bit late," Ferro sniggers. "Your girlfriend gave you the benefit of the doubt for all of ten minutes."

"Stop it!" Claudia cries.

Ferro snaps his fingers. "Damn! There goes my biological warfare theory."

The phone rings again.

Ferro massages his foot. "I could reformulate it. Localized biological warfare. First they took Bologna. Tonight, Parma. Tomorrow, the world."

Tomas covers his ears so as not to hear. "Calm down," Claudia says to comfort him. "Calm down. She'll call again. She'll call again, you'll see. She'll call again as soon as we're out of here. You can call her yourself when we're out of here." She's just drunk the contents of the second coffee chocolate, but it hasn't done her any good. That thick, pasty liquid has made her throat even drier. She feels worse than ever.

"You don't know what you're talking about," Tomas says, and his voice sounds very thin. "You don't know what you're talking about. My life is over. You really don't know what the *fuck* you're talking about. Be quiet, please. Just be quiet."

The phone rings for a third time.

Tomas closes his eyes.

"I need a cigarette," Ferro yells suddenly. "I go crazy if I don't smoke. Don't worry, I'll open the doors myself, I'd like to keep at least one foot intact. Or else I'll smoke in here."

"There's no air in here," Claudia protests.

Ferro ignores her. He searches for his cigarettes and his lighter, and doesn't make any move to open the doors.

"Please," Claudia moans, as the phone rings a fifth time. "We can't breathe. We can't breathe in here. We can't breathe. None of us."

Ferro turns away in annoyance. He puts a cigarette in his mouth and lights it.

Claudia gets up and drags herself to the doors. She looks to Tomas for help, but Tomas is in the abyss.

She tries to open the doors by herself, with all the strength left in her body. Just an inch or two. A little oxygen. Just a little.

Ferro blows out the smoke, and starts humming *Mystery Train* in a hollow voice.

The phone rings one last time, then silence returns to rule the roost.

Hour Six

They aren't speaking. Their palates are rough, their tongues dry. No point in wasting words.

Claudia is breathing softly, in symbiosis with the little ball that's throbbing in her sternum.

There's only one thought in her head. *I want to get out of here I want to get out of here I want to get out of here I want to get out of here I want to get out of here I want to get out of here I want to get out of here I want to get out of here I want to get out of here I want to get out of here I want to get out of here I want to get out of here to get out of here to get out of here to get out of here to get out of here to get out of here*

to get out of here I want to get out of here I want to get out of here I want to get out of here I want to get out of here I want to get out of here I want to get out of here.

In his corner of the elevator, Ferro is listening to the voice of a dead man.

"I don't want any trouble, guys," the dead man is saying.

Ferro laughs, but no one is listening to him.

The voice belongs to the Dealer, their very first guest at the shack in the woods. The Dealer was tied to the chair with a chain round his chest and thighs. The Dentist was there in front of him, with his arms folded. Ferro was a little further behind.

The Dealer had made a stupid decision. He'd chosen as his area of operations the square in front of the Graceland, Ferro's first club – the Pink Cadillac and the Memphis were still to come.

Ferro had tried every way he could to persuade him to move his territory, to shift a few hundred yards, just a few hundred yards. He had even hired vigilantes, but all to no avail: the Dealer had carried on plying his trade and displaying the same arrogant, insolent attitude.

"Well," the Dentist had said one day, "if the law can't help us, I'll have to deal with it myself."

And now here was the Dealer, sitting there in front of them, in the shack, chained to a chair and perfectly lucid, saying over and over, "I don't want any trouble, guys, I don't want any trouble."

He had realized he was in a hopeless situation, of course, but he hadn't realized quite *how* hopeless. The Dentist's magic potions were having their effect, the Dealer was lucid but numb from the neck down. The stupid idiot thought he could still negotiate, that he could get through this somehow or other. He promised he'd move, he wouldn't cause anyone any trouble any more; in fact, he added, he could even work for them, make sure their territory stayed clean. Leave it to him, he said, and no one would ever deal outside the Graceland.

Ferro listened to him incredulously, his eyes wide open, a knot in his stomach. *Doesn't he realize?* he kept asking himself, appalled. *Hasn't he noticed anything? How is that possible?*

The Dentist always had a lot of fun in that kind of situation. "So," he sneered, "you're willing to negotiate. Not so arrogant now, are you? We might even consider letting you go . . . What do you think, partner?"

Ferro nodded mechanically. The Dealer kept repeating, "Yes, yes, I don't want any trouble, guys, just let me go and I'll put in a good word for you, I give you my word of honour." And as he talked, on and on, Ferro couldn't take his eyes off the bucket on the wooden floor next to the chair.

The bucket containing the Dealer's arms.

His feet, sawn off at the ankles.

And most of his intestines.

The Dealer, numb from the neck down, kept repeating, quite lucidly, "I don't want any trouble, guys, I don't want any trouble."

"You want to get out of here," the Dentist concluded, triumphantly. "That's fine, we can talk about it, we're reasonable people."

A surreal trace of hope appeared on the Dealer's face.

"But," the Dentist continued, "before getting out of here you should at least make yourself presentable." He turned to Ferro. "Fetch him the mirror," he said, and added, "The big one."

Ferro brought the mirror, the big one, and placed it just in front of the Dealer's chair.

Many years later, Ferro again savours the taste of metal under his tongue.

He can feel the red mask pushing under the surface of his face, pushing to get out.

177

Hour Eight

0:10 a.m.

The fear of enclosed spaces.
The fear of strangers.
The fear of not being able to breathe.
And last but not least, the ultimate fear.
The dark.

Ten minutes after midnight, the threads which have been stretched to breaking point inevitably snap. Loudly and violently.

"I can't take it any more," Claudia screams hysterically, leaping suddenly to her feet. "I can't take it any more. I can't take it any more. There's no air. I'm suffocating. I'm suffocating."

She sways. She looks at Tomas, who's lying on his side in a corner of the elevator, a human wreck playing with his house keys. "Give me a hand," she implores him, wild-eyed. "Let's open the doors. Let's open the doors. I don't have the strength any more, I can't do it on my own. This isn't right. This isn't bearable."

(The little girl was on her knees, scratching at the bricks, scratching with her little nails.)

(I'm not scared of anything, but this is a bit too much.)

Tomas stands up, silently. He helps her to open the doors, still without a word. Then he goes back and sits down.

Ferro watches them from the back of the elevator, with his yellow, watery eyes. He's doing something weird, something disgusting, chewing his lower lip as if to draw water and sustenance from his own saliva glands.

Claudia sits down between the doors, on the runner. She presses backwards with her back and forwards with her knees, puts her head three inches out of the elevator, and inhales the stagnant, crypt-like air in the elevator shaft, that little bit of air that means all the difference between dying and staying alive. It's worth bearing the pressure of the steel on her bones, on her flesh, it's worth it to breathe that little bit of dead, sluggish air.

Ferro says nothing, does nothing. He just watches her, watches her writhing between the doors, his eyes yellow in the green light.

Then he stops chewing and opens his mouth. His voice echoes through the elevator like a madman's.

"You're good at making yourself useful," he says laboriously, his tongue moving like an old sewing machine. "You're really good at making yourself useful. I think there are ways you could make yourself even more useful."

"Listen," Claudia roars, invigorated by the new air. "If you're about to come out with some other wretched nonsense. If all you're going to do is waste your breath and consume oxygen. Then do us a favour. Just drop it."

Ferro gives a phlegmy laugh and coughs twice. "How well you speak, how good you are, *wretched nonsense, consume oxygen,* how refined you are, how well you speak, no, really, you know how you could make yourself useful, in my opinion?" He coughs again. "You could move that delicate little hand of yours up and down on this boy's wretched little dick, up and down, you know what I mean? And at the same time you could put that refined pink mouth of yours right here between my legs. Taking care not to stick your knee on my poor ankle, if possible. What do you think, signorina? Does the proposition interest you?"

Tomas shows no sign of having heard any of this. He keeps playing absently with his keys.

Claudia looks Ferro in the eyes with all the contempt she's capable of, lucid and recharged with that little bit of air in her lungs. "Listen," she hisses, "that was exactly what I meant when I said you shouldn't waste your breath. If all you can do is talk bullshit like that, you dimwit, why don't you move your own hand up and down on yourself if you want to, maybe it'll calm you down. And when you come, make sure it's against the wall, please." And she turns back to the elevator shaft.

Ferro laughs like a villain in a B-movie and scratches his rough chin. "Oh, very good, very good, signorina," he croons. "Very good, signorina, why don't you wash your mouth out with soap, nice signorina? Why don't you wash your mouth out with soap and then spit it all out, nice signorina? Eh? Why not?"

Claudia looks at him in alarm.

He's losing it. He's losing it completely.

Then Ferro gets to his feet, the whole weight of his body on his left foot, and starts unbuttoning his trousers.

Claudia flinches. "What the fuck are you doing? What the fuck do you think you're doing?"

Ferro sees her alarmed expression, and laughs. "Relax, signorina. I'm peeing. Emptying my bladder. Taking a leak. It happens sometimes. Relax."

And he unleashes a powerful jet of urine against the steel wall. It hits the metal with a sound like a storm beating on a window.

Ah, perfect, the smell was already so bad you couldn't breathe in here. And now this. Great, this was all we needed.

She again looks to Tomas for support, but Tomas is hypnotized by the movement of the keys in his fingers. She searches for Tomas's eyes and instead finds Ferro's. Ferro has done up his trousers.

He has turned to face her.

"Are you looking?" he growls.

"No, I wasn't looking."

"You were looking. You liked it."

"No, I wasn't —"

Before Claudia can finish the sentence, the lights go out.

"Darkness!" the little girl who scratched at the bricks screams. "Darkness! The lights have gone out! I'm scared! I'm not scared of anything, but this is a bit too much!"

Then Claudia regains control, her eyes gradually becoming accustomed to the dark.

Stay calm! The lights went out when the elevator stopped too. Maybe we're about to start up again. Yes. Maybe the lights went out because we're about to start up again!

So get away from the doors, girl! If we're about to start up again, they'll close like a pair of pincers!

Get away from here, before these steel things crush you like a walnut!

Claudia is about to move away from the runner and roll to the side.

But before she can do so, a hundred and seventy-five pounds of sweaty flesh land on top of her.

When the lights went out, a switch went on in Aldo Ferro's mind. It was as if the last thin membrane between him and the Red Mask simply melted like sugar.

He took a step forward in the dark, supporting himself on his good foot.

And threw himself blindly on the girl with green hair.

"Tomas!" Claudia screams, when Ferro crushes her with the full weight of his body. "Tomas! Help!"

That's as much as she can scream, because she can't breathe.

She has a hundred and seventy-five pounds pressing on her lungs.

There's no room to escape.

There's no room to move her arms.

There's no room to move her legs.

The doors are still pressing on her shoulders and knees.

Behind her head, a concrete wall.

In the dark, hands move frantically. Hands defending themselves. Other hands touching. Blocking the door.

"It was bound to happen," the little girl screams inside her head. "It was bound to happen, bound to happen, bound to happen, bound to happen."

"Why did you say the elevator had moved?" Ferro spits,

183

less than an inch from her face. "Why, you dirty bitch? Why did you deceive me? Eh? Why did you say the elevator had moved? Why? Why?"

Ferro is completely different from the comical Elvis lookalike who entered the elevator at five o'clock that afternoon. Hidden in the darkness, his face isn't even his own face any more. It's a mask with an unnatural grin, and eyes as deep and dark as pits to hell.

Claudia inhales the rancid stench of sweat and fear, the breath like a dead man's lashing her face. His breath is in her ears, a convulsive rhythmic panting like that of an ox.

Then Ferro's right hand works its way like a claw under her barmaid's uniform.

No!

The hand grabs a piece of the material, and rips it as if it were tissue paper.

No!

Then it slides up Claudia's left thigh.

Ferro brutally parts her legs with his knees.

This isn't right! I can't defend myself! I don't have room to defend myself! I'm blocked on every side! It isn't right! It isn't right!

I'm powerless. Completely powerless.

She has nothing to hold on to.

She can't fight back, can't get a grip.

The pressure of the doors and Ferro's weight are crushing her poor bones as if they were toothpicks. She can feel his saliva drooling on her neck.

"Tomas!" she gasps, with her last ounce of breath. "Help me! Help me!"

Then, suddenly, she's free.

Ever since he heard the telephone ringing, Tomas has been in retreat from reality. He has become a guest in his own body. The thought of Francesca, alone at the station with her disappointment, is too painful to bear.

And so he has become mesmerized by the slow, hypnotic movement of the keys. He has shut himself up like an egg in the centre of his being, sheltered from the heat and the thirst and the feeling that his lungs are full of petrol. He has let his body carry on existing, mechanically. When the lights went out, he almost didn't notice.

It's only Claudia's cry for help that finally brings him back to reality.

Suddenly alert, he immediately grasps what is happening. In fact he knew it would happen. He's known it ever since he entered the elevator. Ever since he looked into Aldo Ferro's predatory eyes.

He acts instinctively. He gets to his feet in the ink-black elevator, guided by the sound of Ferro's voice screaming something at Claudia.

He's never in his life been in a fight, but now he takes a step in the dark.

In his hand, he's clutching the big heavy key to the basement.

He strikes out blindly, in the direction of the voice.

Ferro is savouring his triumph.

He hears the material tearing like paper. Feels the girl's warm flesh beneath his fingers. Smells the odour of fear.

*Not so tough now, are you, you whore? Not so tough now, now
that I've got you where you were meant to be.*

He spreads her legs with his knees. They yield easily. He's
about to show the bitch who's in charge.

Then, all of a sudden, the world bursts inside his head.

Something has hit him, very suddenly, very unexpectedly,
has hit him on his left ear. It has hit him so hard that
something that should be *outside* now seems to be *inside*.
Where it should never be.

Gurgling with pain, he moves backwards, with his hands
on his ear. A storm is raging in his head; it screams and
blows like the sound of the sea in a shell.

The kid.

It was the kid.

What did he hit me with?

Fucking fairy's broken my eardrum.

It's because the space is too small.

A predator can't move in such a small space.

It doesn't matter.

I'll kill him.

I'll butcher him like an animal.

Tomas feels the iron key hit *something*, maybe a bone, maybe
the skull, he doesn't know. Then Ferro leaps backwards,
brushing against him with his sweaty body. Gurgling like a
turkey less than two feet away from him.

Tomas doesn't move.

What do I do now?

Do I hit him again?

I can't even see him.

What do I do now?

186

A sound in the darkness, only an inch or two from him. Like the click of a jack knife being opened.

Claudia is in shock.

The sudden darkness and Ferro's weight on her

(he wanted to rape me! he would have raped me here, between the doors! he's crazy!)

have broken down some barrier in her brain. All she can think is, *The doors, the doors, I have to keep the doors open, I can't go back inside the elevator, I have to breathe, just breathe, I have to keep the doors open. No, no, forget about the doors, I have to help Tomas, to get away from these fucking doors, we have to attack him together, jump him, I have to move away from the doors, I have to move away from the doors.*

Then there's a sound, in the darkness.

When was the last time she heard that sound?

When she was little and went fishing with her father? Is that possible?

Suddenly she realizes.

A knife, a knife, a knife.

Ferro has a knife, a knife, a knife.

Ferro makes the first thrust blindly, in the darkness, the storm howling in his ear. He misses his target. The blade hits the steel wall, raising sparks in a hiss of metal on metal.

Ferro grinds his teeth.

The second thrust will be the right one.

Tomas feels something pass close to his head, hears a whistling in the air. Instinctively he drops the keys, reaches out his hands in front of him, and in his blindness manages to seize Ferro's wrists. He squeezes as hard as he can.

He hears Ferro grunt and curse four inches from his face.

Oh God.

I'm fighting him.

He's much stronger than me.

He's much bigger than me.

I can't see him but he's here, right here, in front of me.

There are a thousand ways Ferro could free himself from Tomas's weak grip, even with the whole weight of his body shifted onto a single ankle and the hurricane blowing in his broken eardrum. He chooses his favourite.

He locates the boy in the darkness from his breathing. He tenses the muscles of his neck and headbutts him, breaking his nose. The vibrations impact on his own wounded eardrum, adding pain to pain.

All the better.

With the pain comes anger.

With the anger comes hate.

And hate is the fuel that burns in the dark heart of the Red Mask.

When he feels the bone shatter in the centre of his face, Tomas lets out a terrifying scream. He lets go of Ferro's wrists and puts his hands together to protect his broken nose.

He staggers back in the dark.

Now he's defenceless.

A single thrust, the Red Mask thinks in anticipation, *a single thrust to the jugular, sharp, precise. Straight across from ear to ear.*

He primes his body to strike, but there's no room to move, fuck, there's no room in this stupid elevator. Instinctively, he moves his weight onto his right foot.

A stab of pain.

From his foot.

His right foot.

Stabbing. Pain on pain.

"Aaaaaargh!" howls the thing that came into the elevator as Aldo Ferro. Losing his balance, he lashes out blindly.

He's too close to miss his target.

Tomas screams in the darkness.

The blade has hit flesh.

The old leader of the herd, with his sharp, strong teeth, has drawn the first blood. The young male staggers and falls back to the ground in the lair. The female watches the fight anxiously.

The Red Mask welcomes the pain. Pain leads to hate, and hate feeds the fire.

The next thrust, the next thrust will be right to the heart.

Tomas disappears.

There's nothing left of the shy, polite sixteen-year-old, the teenager in love escaping to Northern Europe. When the blade cuts the flesh between his neck and his back,

Tomas escapes in terror to some soft, safe place behind his brain. He collapses, giving way to pure instinct.

What's happening? It's dark. I can't see anything.
  Who's screaming? Who hit who?
  I have to get away from the doors.
  I have to get away from the doors.
  Why aren't they responding?
  My muscles?
  My nerves?
Then a dim light illuminates the scene.

And shows Claudia what she'd have given anything not to see.

Aldo Ferro searches for the lighter in his pocket. Calmly, triumphantly.

Balanced on his left foot and the tip of his right.

He lights the inside of the elevator with the little flame, and savours the scene of his victory.

And the spatters of blood on the steel walls.

Claudia looks at Ferro standing there in front of her, sneering in the lighter flame.

Like the damned in her grandfather's illustrated copy of Dante's *Inferno*. The tombs glowing red in the eternal flames, the ochre tints, the lights flickering like the reflections from a fireplace.

Tomas is lying on the floor in front of Ferro, like a puppet with its strings broken. There's blood on his face, back and chest. His eyes are wide open. His breathing is feverish.

Claudia is in Hell. In Hell.

Ferro bends and puts his right knee on the floor to rest his ankle, watching Claudia out of the corner of his eye, making sure she doesn't try anything.

He goes closer to Tomas, this kid who hurt him with that ridiculous key.

He missed the jugular by an inch or two. It's all the fault of the darkness and the pain in his ankle; he would never ever have missed the target if it wasn't for the darkness and the pain in his ankle. He would have sliced him open like a pig, with a simple twist of the wrist.

"Oh, well," he thinks. "There's plenty of time to remedy that."

He strokes Tomas's Adam's apple with the tip of his knife.

The little steel ball in Claudia's sternum starts to blow a cold wind. Her nerves seem to turn to ice, to become one with the steel that surrounds her.

She's as cold as snow now. She doesn't move. She waits.

Ferro is about to sink the blade into the flesh, but hesitates.

He's just thought of a better idea.

He could leave the boy with the piercing alive for a while longer.

And make him and the girl with green hair play a few games together.

Then he'll make the girl swallow those airs and graces of hers, that *I'm an emancipated woman and I'm not afraid of men* attitude, and then he'll force her to play some very interesting little games with her little friend. It'll be fun to watch.

His mind is made up.

He takes the blade away from Tomas's throat, gives a derisive smile and turns to Claudia.

With the lighter in one hand and the knife in the other.

Humiliated by the Pig in the bar.

Humiliated by the madman in the street.

Humiliated by the man on the bus.

Almost raped by this sweaty monster.

She's breathed filth.

And drunk from a chocolate.

Claudia has endured more than a human should have to endure, and now she's had enough.

With a click, the little steel ball expands, breaking through her ribcage, her nerves, her muscles. Every one of her cells turns to steel, her steel back against the steel doors, her legs of steel holding back doors of steel.

Her muscles tense as the monster stops in front of her. Breathing his carbolic-acid breath all over her.

"Hello, princess," Ferro pants, only an inch or two away from her. He's leaning on the left-hand door with his elbow to support himself, the weight of his body on his left foot, only the tip of the right touching the floor. He twists the knife between the fingers of his right hand. "I'm so sorry I haven't brought any flowers or chocolates. Plus, it's August Bank Holiday Sunday, the cinemas are closed, and we'd have a hard job finding a little restaurant for a candlelit dinner. So I hope you'll forgive me if we skip a few preliminaries in our courtship."

"Wait."

"Or are you the kind of girl who only enjoys it if I play a little with the knife? No problem at all. Tell me where you want me to start and I'll start."

"No, I mean" – and Claudia lowers her voice – "there's no need for anyone to get hurt. If I cooperate, then things could be a lot nicer for both of us."

And she puts her right hand on the buckle of Ferro's belt, just below his bare, sweaty stomach. She softly strokes the buckle, still holding the doors open with her shoulders and knees.

Ferro watches, pleased with those thin, suddenly compliant fingers. He laughs. "Well, well, that's good, carry on. You're a cute little thing, aren't you? Why don't you repeat what you said before, you little slut? Why don't you repeat those sweet words, wait, let me quote from memory, 'You dimwit, why don't you move your hand up and down on yourself, and make sure you come against the wall.' Eh? Why don't you repeat all that, with that little mouth of yours? Go on. Let me hear that. Then I'll tell you something in return."

(Now I've spoiled it all again. The Dentist would never have said anything so vulgar. He was such a good talker, I never learned to be that.)

Claudia looks him right in the eyes, still stroking his belt buckle.

"If you want me to come away from the doors," she says, softly, "then I'll come away from the doors."

193

She tightens her fingers on the buckle.

And pulls it towards her.

With all the strength she has in her arm.

"Take advantage of your opponent's weight against you," her judo teacher used to say. That was before he snuck into her shower and offered to soap her back.

Claudia's right leg moves forward like a spring, rigid and taut.

It hits Ferro's left ankle.

It lifts his left foot from the floor, the foot which is carrying his weight.

At the same time as she pulls with her right arm. With all the strength she has.

A kind of hiccup comes from Ferro's throat as he feels the ground falling away beneath his feet. "Uh?"

He bends forward like a cut tree, a victim of the age-old mechanism of a perfect lever.

Then Claudia rolls away from the doors.

Making herself into as much of a ball as possible.

It all happens in a fraction of a second.

Ferro, pitching forward, waves his hands in the air.

Claudia crouches below him, well away from the runner now.

The steel doors, without her body there to hold them apart, close like a pair of pincers.

On either side of Aldo Ferro's head.

A sound echoes in the elevator.

194

The horrible *splat!* of a ripe melon as it breaks open on the pavement after falling from the seventh floor of a building.

Amateur. Stupid amateur.

The Dentist was the good one of you two. He was the man of action. You were always the copy, the imitator. He would never have let himself be taken in by a girl. You let yourself be taken in by a girl. No one ever lets himself be taken in by a girl, not even in a crummy movie.

This stupid ankle. It's all the fault of this stupid ankle.

And the broken eardrum.

You let yourself be taken in by a girl and a young kid with a piercing. The Dentist would never have cut such a sorry figure.

Get up now. Get up, shift your weight onto your left foot. You have a knife. They don't. Get up. Enough of these games. Tear them to pieces, the two of them.

Wait!

What's happening? The elevator? Is the elevator moving? Is it going down?

I don't understand. Is the elevator going down, or have I melted, am I dripping down through the elevator shaft like petrol?

Look, we've gone down to the tenth floor, look who's here, on the tenth floor, it's Sonja, the barmaid from Lecce, she lives here, imagine that. I was sure she lived in that apartment with the Ligabue poster and the almost double bed, I never realized the apartment was in this building, just imagine.

Alex? Is that Alex on the ninth floor?

I thought I left him in the shack. He's dragged himself all the way here, tied to the chair. Good. He's been really good. Not easy, dragging yourself all the way here tied to a chair. With his face nailed on upside down. He's been good.

The Dentist, look at that, there's the Dentist, on the eighth floor. I thought the Dentist was dead. I thought he was dead, but there he is, on the eighth floor.

And that guy tied to the chair isn't Alex. It's the Dealer.

Well, well, the Dealer hasn't even noticed he's been gutted. He's lost his arms and his feet. Wait till he sees himself in the mirror.

My son, as a baby. He wasn't fat at all when he was a baby. He was beautiful when he was born. God knows how he got to be so fat.

Gloria? Am I marrying Gloria?

Didn't I get married once, to Gloria? She insisted on getting married in church, because her father was such a traditionalist, and yet here we are, getting married on the sixth floor. God knows what her father will say about us getting married on the sixth floor of this building.

This elevator is going down too quickly. Much too quickly. You're about to see that the cables have snapped, fucking hell, we're going to smash into the ground, that's the last straw. Who is that boy kicking the lamp posts in the street? Is it me?

Is that my grandma's kitchen? Why is the table so high? Why does everything look so big?

Oh, fuck, that's it, I knew it, the cables have snapped. We've passed the ground floor, now we're falling into the basement.

It's dark in the basement. It's all dark. You can't see anything.

Have we stopped moving?

Whose voices are these? I know these voices.

What are they saying? That they were waiting for me?

Who are you?

I'm scared.

You there, in the dark. Who are you?

Who are you? I know you.
I'm scared.

And outside the motionless elevator, outside the white twenty-storey tower block, outside the city where the night has turned cool at last, in the shack in the middle of the woods, Alex is looking out at the world through what used to be his mouth. Waiting for the return of the Red Mask.

Since he went mad, two hours ago, he's stopped being afraid of the knife. He's waiting calmly. He's looking at the light of the stars behind the curtains nailed to the windows, and waiting.

Two hours ago, the effects of the dentist's potions wore off. And Alex, deprived suddenly of that subtle mixture of painkillers and sedatives, became aware of what had happened to him. Physically, and mentally.

In one fell swoop, a wave of unbearable pain and the awareness that he had been reduced to a living puppet seared his nerves. He was like a burning light bulb, that was his last conscious thought. Just a burning light bulb. A few particularly nice synapses abdicated and said goodbye to the world, and Alex, quite simply, went completely mad.

Now he's waiting for the man in the red mask.

The man said he was going to castrate him with his knife. That was many hours ago. Alex remembers it well, he remembers those words reaching him through the haze of sedatives and painkillers. But the man in the red mask hasn't come back.

And for the last few minutes there's been a strange noise, upstairs. Like an animal rooting around in a world of objects it doesn't know and doesn't understand.

197

"A wild boar," a little voice says from out of the amorphous mush that is Alex's mind. "Maybe a wild boar got in, and in a while it'll find its way down here."

"How the fuck did a wild boar get in through the window upstairs?" another little voice asks. "Do you know? Do I know? I don't know. Do you know? Do you prefer to be eaten by a wild boar or cut to ribbons a piece at a time by the Red Mask? You choose. This is the card, here's the queen, here's the queen, where's the queen?"

From time to time, in waves, fragments of rationality come together like the pieces of a jigsaw puzzle behind that upside-down face. And another little voice says, "Maybe there's no animal rooting around upstairs, maybe it's only the nail that's embedded in your forehead, the one on the right, not the one on the left, the one on the right has been driven further in. Maybe that noise you hear is nothing but the nail, the nail squeaking against your skull."

In those momentary flashes of rationality, Alex thinks of rocking on the chair until he falls forward, face first. And then once he's fallen face first, beating his head against the floorboards, so as to drive the nails deeper in. And get it over with. Before the wild boar. And before the man in the red mask.

But, however hard he tries, Alex can't move the chair. Not even a fraction of an inch.

The moment of rationality dissolves like steam. It rises in thin clouds up above the light bulb, and out beyond the shack, and away, far away.

And Alex waits in the centre of the room, once again pitifully, fortunately, completely mad.

*   *   *

In the deserted square in front of the station in Parma, a girl named Francesca has just stopped crying her eyes out.

She's waiting for a night bus which may never arrive. She has a suitcase beside her, and she keeps repeating, "Why? Why did he do something like that to me? Why? Why?"

When all the passengers got off the 8:54 train and there wasn't a sign of Tomas, she didn't lose faith. She called him on his mobile and found it was switched off, then she called his home and no one answered, but still she didn't lose faith.

Tomas might have missed the train. The battery on his mobile might have gone. His parents might have come back unexpectedly. There were a thousand possible explanations for his absence.

She waited for the second train from Bologna, still full of hope.

But Tomas wasn't on the second train either.

Or the third.

Or the fourth.

Francesca constantly checked the mobile, hoping for a missed call, a text message, some sign, some explanation. She called Tomas a thousand times, and a thousand times she heard the answer *The number is currently unobtainable.*

And the trains came and went, passed one after the other. And the station started to fill up with horrible faces, dazed with the heat, drunks wandering in the damp-laden evening.

At midnight she gave up.

She dragged her suitcase out of the station, sobbing, cursing that bastard Tomas.

Why? Why did you deceive me? Why did you do something like that to me? Why?

Now she's waiting for a night bus, at half past midnight on August Bank Holiday Sunday. In a deserted city, surrounded by shuffling zombies, dealers lurking in the shadows.

Finally, she sighs and walks away from the bus stop. She drags her suitcase across the square in front of the station, towards the bridge over the River Parma, its bed dried by the heat. She'll walk home. That too is her fate.

As long as she gets there before her parents. She *has* to get there before her parents.

Before her mother and father find the note on the table.

Before they come home, furious because they've just been refused the loan they were desperate to get, and find the note saying: *I'm leaving home, don't try to find me, I'll be fine.*

Francesca is sure of one thing. If her father reads the note, his eyes will pop out of his head, and his first impulse will be to strangle his daughter. And if at that moment his daughter comes in through the door, well, there's no doubt what he'll do. The Supermaxihero will grab hold of her and throttle her right there in the living room.

That's why Francesca starts walking faster, as fast as she can. The suitcase is heavy; it thumps loudly on the pavement, echoing like a firecracker in the silence of the night.

She crosses the bridge, repeating to herself, "Bastard. Bastard. Bastard." And then she tenses.

She can hear footsteps behind her.

Francesca turns her head slightly, a frightened prickling at the back of her neck.

There's a man behind her. He's walking slowly, the glow of a cigarette clearly visible in the darkness.

Francesca's heart leaps into her throat. She walks even faster, tightening her grip on her mobile. What's the number for the police? Is there a bar open, somewhere she can take refuge? The city looks like it's survived a nuclear winter: lights out, doors closed, shutters down. Not even a car passing, not even a drunk on a bicycle, no one who can help her in case of emergency.

There are only those two noises beneath the stars. The suitcase being laboriously dragged along the pavement, and the slow, constant footsteps of the stranger at the end of the street.

Shit. Shit. Shit. If this guy comes any closer, I'll leave the case and run like the wind. But shit, I've always been a slow runner. I'm always among the last in the cross-country races, me and the fat girl. This was all I needed. It's all the fault of that bastard.

I hate you, Tomas.

I hate you.

We should have been across the border by now. Instead of which, I'm here, in this deserted city, dragging a suitcase, watching the glow of a stranger's cigarette behind me.

I hate you. I swear I hate you.

Another hundred yards, and the sound of the stranger's footsteps is replaced by the creak of a door opening. Francesca turns her head again. The stranger is calmly entering his building.

201

Francesca can breathe again. She relaxes her grip on her mobile, and continues her slow, interminable walk. Halfway there, the night bus passes her.

She doesn't even get angry. She doesn't have the strength any more.

She's reached home.

It was all a delusion, thinking she could escape from here. All that's happened is that she's fallen to earth with a dull thud.

Before entering the building, she makes one last attempt. She calls Tomas's mobile for the last time, closes her eyes, and repeats, "Answer, answer, answer, answer, you bastard, I hate you, I hate you, I hate you."

But, as usual, the number called is not currently obtainable.

So Francesca sighs and drags the suitcase up the stairs, on the way to meet her destiny.

Please don't let my parents be back yet. Please don't let them be back, IbegyouIbegyouIbegyouIbegyou.

She reaches the landing.

She searches for her keys.

And that's when she hears the voices on the other side of the door. Her mother and father.

They're already back. They're inside the apartment, shouting and screaming in the middle of the night.

She props her suitcase on the landing and sits down on the top step, her arms round her knees.

She doesn't have the courage to go inside. She doesn't know what to do. She doesn't know where to go.

So she sits there, even when the lights go out on the

stairs. She sits there in the dark, without knowing what to do or where to go, listening to that terrible screaming and shouting on the other side of the door.

In the Moroccan desert, south of Erfoud, surrounded by dunes, Bea is looking up at the stars.

During the first weeks of shooting, she managed to communicate with Claudia at least once a day. They said really sweet things to each other in those first weeks of being separated, without a trace of irony, things like "If we look at the same star at the same time we'll know we're thinking of each other," really sappy things like that.

But Bea doesn't have time for e-mails and phone calls any more, now that the shooting has got really tough. The director is squeezing her dry, and not just him, the fencing master, the head stuntman, the horses, the fucking camels, they're all killing her, physically and mentally. Especially the camels.

She looks up at the sky, searches for their star, hers and Claudia's, but however hard she tries she can't find it. The constellations seem different, alien, when she's out here, surrounded by dunes. Everything seems different when you're surrounded by dunes.

She looks at the distant trailers, over towards the horizon.

Better get some sleep, she thinks. *Tomorrow's going to be a madhouse. All those scenes on the camels, the fucking camels, that disgusting stuff they spit. Repulsive animals.*

She brushes the sand from her light cotton trousers.

She gets back in the car.

And drives slowly over the sand, under the starry sky.

***

Two hours by air from the Moroccan desert, on the outskirts of a city that's been baked by the sun all through a long day, Claudia is breathing so heavily, she's almost hyperventilating. Her heart is beating so hard, it's as if it's trying to burst through her chest. Her chest itself is crushed under Aldo Ferro's now motionless body. The lighter has fallen from that lifeless hand. It's dark again.

Slowly, swallowing her saliva, which tastes acid, she slides out from under that mass of dead, cold flesh. The smell in the elevator is unbearable now.

Claudia searches for the lighter, groping with her hand on the bubbled rubber. She touches things, viscous, liquid, soft, flabby things,

(I don't want to know what I'm touching. I don't want to know what I'm touching. I don't want to know what I'm touching)

the blade of the knife, from which she recoils immediately.

Just when she's convinced that the lighter has fallen down the elevator shaft, she finds it. In a pool of some horrible, thick liquid.

She picks it up. Her fingers are shaking uncontrollably. Her whole body is rocked by terrible shudders.

She lights the flame, and the elevator is illuminated.

Ferro is in a ridiculous, unnatural position. He's like someone who's put his head through the oval hole on a sheet of cardboard to have his photo taken with his face on the body of a cowboy or a bodybuilder.

204

Except that his arms hang limply by his sides. His knees graze the floor.

His head is crushed between the doors.

And his blood is dripping rhythmically onto the runner, like a leaking tap.

"Is he dead?" Tomas gasps.

Claudia turns. Tomas is lying motionless at the back of the elevator, looking at her with empty, watery eyes.

"Yes," she replies, then collapses, overcome by the tension and the stench of excrement, blood and sweat. She vomits between the folded country-style shirt and Ferro's right boot, the one he took off after the accident with his ankle. She throws it all up, chocolate, coffee, gastric juices, shaking violently, her uniform torn along the left thigh. The little metal ball that made her strong and determined has gone back into the alien universe it came from.

At last, Claudia stirs herself. She wipes her mouth with Ferro's shirt, picks up the Bruce Springsteen T-shirt from the floor, and tears it into three with her free hand and her teeth. She's trying to stay lucid, trying not to think that with every movement she makes she's brushing against a corpse with a smashed head, touching it with her bare legs. Making an effort not to think about that, she kneels in front of Tomas and binds his wound as best she can with the improvised bandages. The thin black material is immediately soaked with blood.

She tries to tear pieces of material from Ferro's shirt with her bare hands, but can't do it. So she picks up the knife from the floor and starts cutting, in silence. While Tomas watches her, smiling sadly.

Claudia makes an effort to ignore the smell of all these

things that ought to be *inside* and instead are *outside*: blood, gastric juices, excrement. All the things that ought to be *inside* and instead are *outside*, whereas she ought to be outside and instead is still stuck inside, unavoidably inside, God knows for how much longer.

"You have to stay awake," Claudia's voice is saying from some corner of the universe. "You have to stay awake, awake, awake, *awake*." Her voice is as soft as honey, it flows down through his auditory canals and echoes in his skull and vibrates all the way down to his throat, but his shoulder is burning with pain, and so Tomas directs the vibrations into darker territory, guides it and pilots it like a rocket floating in empty space out on the edges; you have to be on the lookout in empty space out on the edges, Tomas says to himself, because it's in empty space out on the edges that the shapeless bees live, and the shapeless bees in the configuration known as Mark V make an impressively loud noise and form a solid mass that can cut a man's neck like a knife, you really have to be on the lookout for the shapeless bees.

"Don't faint again," Claudia is repeating, "you have to hold on to reality, you have to hold on to reality, tell me something, talk to me, what's your father's name?"

A new little mouth opens in the darkness in the middle of Tomas's head, a mouth that laughs and says, in a voice that sounds like someone chewing nails and shards of glass, "I don't even remember my father's name, I don't remember any of that, I have other things to do, I fought the monster and now the monster is dead, but when his head came away from his body his poisoned blood covered

206

me, all black and thick, and now I'm dying too, which doesn't seem right; I should be in Amsterdam right now, and if I agree to stay a few more hours in this elevator you could at least be kind enough to make sure I don't bleed so much."

"What's your father's name?" Claudia asks again. "Tomas, Tomas, hold on to reality, stay awake, don't leave me alone, Tomas, what's your father's name? Tell me your father's name."

The little mouth in Tomas's head replies, "I don't remember my father's name," and he must have said it very loudly, because the sound comes out through the bigger mouth on Tomas's face above the knife wound and Claudia hears him because she says, "What do you mean, you don't remember?"

And the little mouth repeats, "I don't remember, I don't remember."

And Claudia says, "What about your mother, what's your mother's name?"

And the little mouth replies, "I don't remember, I don't remember, I don't remember, leave me alone, I'm fine here."

.

Interlude: Wilmo

Wilmo Chiodi also liked capturing lizards when he was a child. He would take them by the tail, stick them in a mayonnaise jar, and film their struggle for life with his toy camera. The last lizard that stayed alive was rewarded with its freedom.

Wilmo Chiodi lived in a cluster of hotels, amusement arcades and beach umbrellas flung down at random on the coast of Emilia-Romagna. A little town that only came alive from May to September, then sank back into the deep sleep of a very long winter. His parents were the owners of the Pensione Miranda, peopled from May to September by German tourists, families with small children, and old couples in search of sun, sea and relaxation. Wilmo would help his parents in the dining room, taking orders for bottled water and wine.

At the end of September, when the sunbeds and the beach umbrellas were folded up and put away until May, when the hotels emptied and the town became like a ghost ship, Wilmo gave free rein to his imagination. The German ladies were kinds and generous with their tips, and at the end of the summer Wilmo put aside all the money he had made during the season. One day, with all those tips, he would buy a cine camera. And then he would put on film all the wonderful images that went through his head during those long days spent watching the rain falling on the icy waves.

Whenever he felt as if he was dying in that horrible, muffled nothingness, Wilmo jumped on his moped and rode to Rimini. Six miles along the wet sea road, the water and sky forming one grey stain as he sped by. He would leave the moped in a side street off the Corso Augusto, and go to warm his bones and his soul in his favourite art house cinema.

He was learning.

He might see a restored copy of *King Kong*, for example, and marvel at Willis O'Brien's stop-motion animation. He could spend a whole afternoon there, watching four films in a row, with his student discount card, alone in the deserted auditorium.

He was learning.

On those afternoons he spent in a run-down art house cinema destined to close not long afterwards, Wilmo Chiodi already had his destiny mapped out in his head.

After finishing high school, Wilmo moved to Bologna to do an Arts, Music and Drama degree. He went to live with an uncle of his, on the very edge of the city, where it met the countryside, in a maze of streets named after former presidents of the Republic.

During those first months at university, Wilmo learned to live with the noise of bulldozers and cranes. On the other side of the street, two huge tower blocks were going up.

Two identical tower blocks.

Wilmo saw them taking shape and growing, rising majestically above the terraces of low reinforced concrete houses with their identical blue balcony railings.

He prepared for his first exams to the accompaniment of excavators roaring, cement mixers rumbling, and bricklayers shouting on the scaffolding.

And then, at an exam, he met Walter.

Hour Nine

Claudia is on her knees in the few inches at her disposal. She has torn another strip off her uniform to use as a bandage, but the blood just keeps gushing out, it keeps gushing out and she really doesn't know what to do. She's afraid that Tomas will bleed to death, and she doesn't know how to prevent that. She's terrified of being alone in this tomb of plastic and steel, alone with two corpses. She's afraid of going crazy, here in the elevator.

Whenever she makes the slightest movement, she brushes against Ferro's body. Impossible to avoid that dead flesh.

The smell in the elevator is unbearable. The air is like a swamp, it penetrates the brain in thin needles. So many small, thin needles.

Claudia closes her eyes very tightly.

Tomas is alternating moments of complete oblivion and others of semi-consciousness. When he opens his mouth the words come out in a hoarse, painful drawl.

"Claudia?"

"Quiet. I'm trying to sleep."

"This isn't a normal blackout. A blackout doesn't last this long."

"What do you mean?"

"Ferro was right. Something's happened outside. Everyone's dead. Everyone. There's nothing outside any more."

"Wait!" Claudia cries. "It's moving!"

"It isn't moving."

"Yes, it is, it's moving! Can't you feel it? The elevator. It's going down. Can't you feel it? It's going down!"

"It isn't going down."

"It is, it's going down, you idiot! It's moving! We're saved! We're saved!"

They wait in silence, concentrating on every vibration. For twenty interminable minutes, Claudia remains as alert as a jungle cat.

Then she collapses to the floor, all her strength gone.

Interlude: Wilmo and Walter

Just as the Earth holds the Moon in thrall and in its turn the Moon influences moods and tides, so Wilmo and Walter started to orbit around each other.

Wilmo was like a volcano, his brain constantly on the boil, a man with more ideas than he could possibly realize.

Walter, well, Walter didn't have ideas, he wasn't brilliant, he wasn't intelligent. But he was the son of Mr Fix-It, and that was enough.

When they met, Walter introduced himself with his full name. And his surname inevitably recalled the name of a major TV personality who was known to all Italians, someone who for thirty years had had an huge influence on the world of television, but not only on the world of television, a genuine Mr Fix-It.

On hearing the surname, Wilmo couldn't help remarking on it. Well aware that Walter had probably heard the same remark every fucking day of his life.

So he asked him, with a smile, "You're not related to . . . ?"

With unexpected candour, Walter cheerfully replied, "Of course. He's my father."

And Wilmo looked at him wide-eyed.

In his head, gate after gate was opening towards the future. Boundless horizons, endless prospects for glory.

He had the opportunity to become the friend – not just

the friend, the brother, the soulmate – of the son of Mr Fix-It. The man who for thirty years had been on first-name terms with the politicians who competed for an invitation onto his show. The man who, with one phone call, could either cut short a career for good or, on the contrary, make sure it really took off.

He tried not to let his joy be too obvious when he shook the hand of this gateway to infinite possibilities and said calmly, "How do you do? I'm Wilmo Chiodi."

Walter was a tall, sprightly young man, with red cheeks and a mass of perennially unkempt hair.

"I want to follow my own path without having to rely on my name!" he would always say. "I'd rather be unloading crates of fruit in a market than ask my father for help. I'm a creative person, I have to make it on my own merits!"

Wilmo would listen to these pompous declarations and smile, thinking, *Yes, yes, of course, absolutely.*

He would always involve Walter – big, good-hearted Walter – in his projects, and Walter never suspected for a moment that all he was getting was the dregs. Wilmo treated him like an equal, made him feel like half of a duo. Whenever he told him about an idea for a short film, Walter's contribution never went any further than an admiring, "Yes, yes, that's great." But, cleverly, Wilmo would always say *our* film, *our* project, always invite his suggestions. Walter would come up with a few paltry ideas, and Wilmo would welcome them, but in words only, never dreaming of actually using them. When the project was finished, Wilmo would say, happily, "We were good, weren't we, partner? We did a good job, didn't we, partner?"

In his innocence, Walter wouldn't even notice that there was almost nothing of his left in the finished product.

All through their university years, Wilmo and Walter were like Siamese twins. They both graduated with honours – Walter's slipshod thesis arousing unjustified, indeed suspect, enthusiasm during its discussion – and as soon as they had graduated they decided to dip their toes in the turbulent waters of show business.

Wilmo dreamed of making it in feature films, but he also knew he had to be realistic, a pragmatist through and through. It was too good an opportunity to pass up: Walter's friendship, and the support of the great puppet-master, working in the shadows, opening all doors for his son. Not to exploit a channel like that, well, it would have been a kind of self-mutilation.

So he made up his mind: he would make a name for himself on TV, putting down solid roots in that world. Once established, he would make the great leap when the moment was right.

Wilmo was the brains, Walter the key.

Soon afterwards, true to the wonderful world of elves and fairy godmothers inside Walter's head, a big player in TV contacted them. *By chance*, he said, he had come across their semi-underground short films, had appreciated their *visionary force*, and wanted to meet these two remarkable young film-makers. It was complete and utter bullshit, but Walter reported it to Wilmo word for word, full of enthusiasm and convinced it was all true.

It never even occurred to him that maybe, just maybe, his father had made a couple of phone calls.

It never even occurred to him that, by a strange coincidence, the big player in question worked for the network of which his father was the director.

He never suspected a thing.

Wilmo knew of course, as he smiled his beatific smile. But he didn't care. His ideas were assuming concrete form at last.

They went straight to Milan for that interview that was nothing but a charade, Walter repeating like a broken record, "My father doesn't even know, think how surprised he'll be if I meet him in the corridor, he doesn't know a thing," and Wilmo thinking, *Yes, of course, just fancy that.*

During the car journey, Wilmo worked out an idea for a show – their show, of course – to propose to the network. He explained it in detail to Walter, and Walter contributed the usual "Yes, yes, wonderful!" and a title for the show. A lousy, jarring title.

Walter emerged from the interview that was nothing but a charade brimming with dumb enthusiasm. "Did you see how impressed he was by our project?" he chirped.

As if it were an everyday occurrence for two recent Arts, Music and Drama graduates without any references to be contacted merely on the basis of two short underground movies, to put forward a far from sure-fire project, and get it accepted just like that, in such a casual way.

An everyday occurrence.

Of course it was.

If you were the son of Mr Fix-It.

* * *

Anyway, the project got under way. With the lousy title *Agreed Statement*, thirty-five twenty-minute episodes, given the off-peak time slot of eleven at night.

Wilmo's idea was simple, brilliant and cheap.

Walter and a couple of sound technicians would position themselves on the balcony of a small apartment block on the outskirts of Milan, a balcony just above a set of traffic lights. Wilmo would be half hidden in a side street, sitting at the wheel of a car with the engine on.

As soon as a lone car appeared and stopped at the lights, Wilmo would come out of the side street and crash into it. When the driver got out, Wilmo would confront him, as bold as brass, claiming to be in the right. What happened after that, Walter would record from the balcony.

Sociologically speaking, the idea yielded fascinating results. The unwitting victims usually reacted by screaming abuse and making frantic phone calls to the traffic police. Then all was revealed, the camera crew showed themselves on the balcony, and Wilmo shook the person's hand and guaranteed to compensate him or her for any damage.

Wilmo proved to be a natural. His Buster Keaton-like expression in situations that could have got very nasty turned out to be one of the best things in the show.

Without batting an eyelid, he swallowed tons of insults, weeping by hysterical women, even a headbutt between his eyes from a man who went off the deep end in the sixth episode. He showed everyone his scar, proudly, as if it were a medal received for valour in the field.

The real disaster came in the ninth episode.

When he met the young lawyer.

* * *

The morning of the disaster began like any other morning. Walter and the sound technicians took up their usual position on the balcony. Wilmo was in his car, with the engine on, waiting for his victim.

The lights had just turned red when the black Volvo appeared at the end of the street. Wilmo had time to notice a girl behind the windscreen, in the front passenger seat, before he released the clutch and moved forward. Aiming for the number plate of the Volvo, which had by now stopped at the lights.

By this stage his technique was well established. He braked suddenly, making sure the tyres screeched a bit for effect, and then crash! Metal on metal, headlights smashed. He got out, wearing his usual stony-faced expression, ready to blame the other driver.

But this time a real madman got out of the jet-black Volvo.

The madman was a distinguished looking thirty-something, well dressed, with short hair, a neatly trimmed goatee beard, a black designer shirt. His eyes were bulging, the veins in his neck swollen, his voice like that of an insane person.

He started screaming, insulting him, accusing him of ruining the Volvo. Before Wilmo could say a word, he grabbed him by the throat.

Wilmo didn't yield to the temptation to give the game away immediately. After all, the most watched episode of *Agreed Statement* had been the one where he'd been headbutted between the eyes, and if the audience wanted to see a little blood, well, for his show, for his dream, Walter was prepared to make sacrifices.

And so he continued to deny the obvious, still incredibly stony-faced. "Just calm down now," he gasped, as the madman squeezed his throat. "Sign the agreed statement and I'll accept full responsibility for the accident."

That was when the madman really flew off the handle. He let fly with a torrent of threats, threats involving certain powerful friends who could crush Wilmo with a phone call, powerful friends who'd be more than ready to come to his aid. He was so mad with rage, so totally out of his head, he even mentioned the names of these friends of his.

Wilmo had time to realize that maybe, just maybe, things were taking a nasty turn. That maybe it was better to end it then and there.

Until a volley of punches to the stomach deprived him of both breath and consciousness.

What happened next, Wilmo only discovered later. Walter and the sound technicians had waved their arms from the balcony, yelling "This is a TV show! This is a TV show!"

Unexpectedly, this had only made the madman even angrier. He had screamed to them to stop filming and give him the tape, while the girl in the Volvo covered her face, and Wilmo vomited blood onto the road.

In the hospital, a white-faced Walter told him what they had found out.

The madman was a go-getting young lawyer, son of a rising politician. With friends in high places, very high places indeed. So high, he really could have called on the names he had screamed in Wilmo's face when he didn't know he was being filmed.

Who the girl in the Volvo was, no one even dared to imagine.

The safety net provided by Walter's father only partly worked this time. Wilmo and Walter had stumbled into a very murky swamp indeed, the same swamp from which Mr Fix-It had drawn sustenance for the past thirty years.

Agreed Statement was cancelled after the eighth episode, officially because of low ratings. Wilmo and Walter made no objection. No objection at all.

They realized that in fact they had been lucky.

Very, very lucky.

If the safety net hadn't saved the programme, at least it had let them down gently. Walter's father came clean to his son – dropping his paper-thin disguise – and laid down drastic conditions for their return to work. Walter thanked him, then went to the hospital to tell Wilmo everything.

"My father says he'll give us a second chance," he said, "but that we have to come back with something really good. Something rock-solid. Something that gets such good ratings, nobody will be able to argue with them." He looked imploringly at Wilmo with his usual good-natured expression, absolutely incapable of coming up with a brilliant idea himself.

"What shall we do, Wilmo? What shall we come up with?" he whispered in a way which meant *"I'm in your hands."*

Wilmo closed his eyes.

And started to think.

Of something good.

Something really good.

Hour Ten

The flame from the lighter has been dead for an hour, but Claudia isn't afraid of the dark. She's too busy remembering the words of a song. She's sitting there, with her fists on her temples, concentrating hard.

There was a time, a while back, when she got it into her head to learn the rudiments of the guitar, with the help only of her brother's untuned Clarissa, a little manual of chords, and a Vasco Rossi songbook. She never got beyond plucking a few notes of this one song, though she always gets the words mixed up. She starts to sing it in the darkness, in a weak voice, and gets as far as the point where she starts to forget the words. Then she gives up and asks for help.

"Tomas? How do the words of *Albachiara* go? Does *in your thoughts* or *in your problems* come first? I remember how it goes on the guitar, C, G, A minor, that I remember, but I've forgotten the words. What comes first, *in your problems* or *in your thoughts?*"

"I don't know."

"It doesn't matter. Sing it with me. Let's just sing it and see how it comes out."

Claudia's voice is like the sad howling of a coyote with the desert in its throat. When the song gets to the thoughts or problems hurdle, she lets it die without any regrets.

Hour Eleven

"Claudia? Are you asleep?"

"Tomas? Is that you?"

"No."

"Who are you?"

"You know who I am."

"No, I don't know. I'm trying to sleep, Tomas is half-conscious, and you're dead, with your head between the doors. So try to stay dead and fuck off."

"I'm sorry you met me like this, Claudia. I wasn't always a bad person."

"Come on, then. Tell me a funny story. Tell me how you almost raped me and made mincemeat of Tomas because your mother made you lick your dirty nappies. Make me laugh. I could do with a laugh."

"No, really. It's a pity you met me like this. I considered myself a rebel when I was at school. I hated my father, I hated what he'd become, a ghost in a vest lying on a couch. A worm who didn't give a shit for my mother, who spent all his money in bars and on the same toothless whore he'd been going to see for the past twenty years. He used to walk around at night smashing street lamps."

"Yes, yes, I can imagine, what a sad story. All right, I understand you, I forgive you. You did the right thing stabbing Tomas, the poor boy's lying here bleeding like a pig, but it's all the fault of your old man who went with whores. OK. You're forty years old and you haven't yet got over the trauma of your father going with whores. That's perfectly reasonable. So maybe it was better this way. Maybe you're better off between those doors, with your brain dripping down the elevator shaft. What do you think?"

"You know something, Claudia? I took part in a competition once. An Elvis lookalike competition."

"Don't tell me."

"I trained so hard for that competition, I prepared *Can't Help Falling in Love*. I rehearsed in front of the mirror, with a tape recorder. I was perfect. Absolutely perfect. Well, I turned up for the competition, which was being held in a crummy little dance hall in the Bassa, and I was as excited as a child, I went to the toilet five times I was so nervous, and at the last moment they changed my song. Can you believe it? The four competitors before me had all chosen *Can't Help Falling in Love*, so they changed my song. It hit me very hard."

"I can imagine. Terrible business. Heart-rending."

"I had to improvise, I did *Suspicious Minds* but I hadn't rehearsed it, you see, I wasn't ready. I came twelfth. After all the time I spent preparing, after all those rehearsals in front of the mirror with the tape recorder, I came twelfth."

"My heart bleeds. Now you've unburdened yourself, please, will you just do me a favour? Go back in the dark and stay dead? Please?"

"I would have won, if they'd let me sing *Can't Help Falling in Love*. I would have won. I'm sure of it."

"FUCK OFF!" Claudia screams at the top of her voice. She jumps to her feet, and her knees squeal with the pain. "I DON'T GIVE A FUCK ABOUT YOUR SHITTY COMPETITION! BURN IN HELL! YOU'RE DEAD, SO STAY DEAD! BURN IN HELL! BURN IN HELL!"

From the dark no voice answers her. Only Tomas's watery coughing, a couple of inches away.

Hour Twelve

"Tomas?" Claudia whispers in the darkness, her head as clear and smooth as a stone in a river.

"Hm?"

"Who were you supposed to be meeting at the station in Parma? Who did you have an appointment with at the station in Parma?"

"No one. I wasn't supposed to be meeting anyone at the station in Parma."

"What the fuck are you talking about? Of course you were supposed to be meeting someone at the station in Parma. You said your life was about to change, that everything depended on that meeting at the station in Parma. That you had to see someone at the station in Parma, at eight fifty-four, I remember that very well, you mentioned eight fifty-four, I'm sure of that. Who were you supposed to be meeting at eight fifty-four at the station in Parma?"

"No one. I don't know anyone in Parma."

Claudia shakes her head. "All right. Convince yourself you don't know anyone at the station in Parma. Just move your tongue as if it were a piece of dead meat, just tell yourself all those beautiful stories. Tell me one too. Tell me a story to pass the time, because in here time never seems to pass; you could still tell me a story before they come and get us out of here, I really think you could."

"I don't know any stories."

"TELL ME A STORY! MAKE ONE UP!"

Tomas spits out a little blood, then swallows.

"I'll tell you the story of Princess Mycomandrya. It's a very, very, very nice story. Listen." He coughs to clear his throat. "There was a knight in armour. He was searching for Princess Mycomandrya, because a sorcerer had kidnapped her and was planning to marry her and make her the queen of the toads. The knight was searching for her in order to free her, and also to marry her himself, I guess. The story doesn't say so but we can assume it." Tomas takes a deep breath, which makes a dull rumble. "The sorcerer had hidden Princess Mycomandrya in a very deep cave. The only way to get to that cave was through a tunnel carved out of the rock."

"Is this the story about the worm in the mountain?"

"No. This is a different tunnel. Listen. The knight in armour went into the tunnel and started to crawl on his stomach, gripping the sides with his fingers, clawing at the bare rock with his nails."

"Didn't the armour have gloves? Why did he have to claw at the rock with his nails if the armour had metal gloves?"

"He couldn't get a grip on the rock with those stubby metal fingers. And so he crawled through the dark tunnel for days on end, with the thirst burning his throat. If only he had water, the knight thought. If he had water everything would be fine, he would get out of the tunnel, he would get to the cave."

"And did he find water?"

"No. He heard a frightening roar, like a landslide, and the tunnel closed behind him. But the knight carried on his way, until he got to the narrow bit."

"What narrow bit?"

"It was a little further on. The tunnel narrowed slightly. Only for an inch or two, just a fold in the rock, but enough to stop him going any further. If he hadn't been in armour, he would have been able to get through."

"So he took off his armour."

"He tried, but he didn't have room to move his arms. He twisted and turned and struggled with that metal cage, but however hard and however long he tried there was no way in the world he could take the armour off. No way. No way at all."

Claudia feels a shiver, like a tarantula climbing up her spine and over the back of her neck and into her green hair. "So what happened then?"

"He tried to break the armour with his fingers until he'd reduced them to little stumps. Then he tried to dig through the rock with his teeth. He couldn't believe he'd been buried alive because of those few inches, just a few inches, he couldn't believe it. He dug with his teeth until he wore out his gums. In the end, his mind sank into a deep well of madness."

"That's horrible. It's a horrible story."

"They say he's still down there. That on nights when there's no wind, you can hear him screaming from the bowels of the earth."

"That's horrible. Horrible. HORRIBLE." Claudia's voice is shrill, like that of a witch. "Why did you tell me that story? Eh? WHY DID YOU TELL ME THAT STORY?"

She digs her nails into Tomas's cheeks, buries them in his skin, grinding her teeth until they squeak. She pushes his head against the steel wall behind him.

Tomas doesn't react. He is hypnotized by the screeching of her teeth in the dark.

Interlude: Three Lizards in a Jar

The red-grey light of dawn touches a blue Transit van, parked with two wheels in the road and two on the pavement in the not yet very distinct shadow of the tower block.

Inside the Transit van, Walter is bouncing about like a crazed electron. Wilmo, on the other hand, is sitting in front of the monitor, calmly smoking a cigarette.

"We're criminals," Walter stammers incoherently, his eyes red and hollow. "That's what we are, criminals. We thought we were artists but we aren't artists, we're criminals, we're both criminals."

"Calm down."

"What do you mean, calm down? Don't you realize? We'll end up in prison! In fucking prison! Don't you realize? We'll end up in fucking prison!"

"Calm down," Wilmo says again, blowing out smoke. "We won't end up in prison. We just have to play our cards right. We just have to bend the truth a little. If we play our cards right, we can come out of this smelling of roses."

He goes back to watching Claudia babbling to herself in the middle of the screen.

Lit by the infrared rays that pierce the darkness.

Knowing they couldn't afford to make a mistake, that their future depended on this show, Wilmo planned everything down to the last detail.

After the usual couple of phone calls from Mr Fix-It, the network offered total logistical and technical support. The fake maintenance team installed hidden miniature remote-controlled cameras in the elevator, disconnected the alarm, set up a screening device to neutralize any mobile phones. Plus a few tricks to liven things up, like the altered doors.

When everything was ready, the ball was in Walter and Wilmo's court.

They put the Out of Order sign in front of the other elevator, in order to make sure the unwitting participants went to the prearranged location. Then they set up camp in the control booth inside the Transit van.

And they waited for two people to enter the elevator at the same time. Two people of the opposite sex, maybe. If something juicy developed, it would certainly be appreciated by the target audience.

They had chosen August Bank Holiday Sunday as a time when there wouldn't be much movement in the building and they could work in peace. Although, obviously, waiting for two people when everywhere was deserted, there was a risk that the two people would never appear. In the early hours of the afternoon, the only person to appear on camera was an old woman who came out of the garage, wiping the sweat off her face with a handkerchief, went up in the elevator alone, and disappeared. No one else.

There was a risk that things would stay that way for quite a while. It didn't matter. Wilmo and Walter were prepared to camp out in the Transit van for as long as it took.

Even if it took a week or a month, they wouldn't let this last opportunity go by.

Then, at about five in the afternoon, a boy with a piercing appeared on the camera in the entrance hall.

He was opening the main door to a girl with green hair.

For the first time in his life, Wilmo found himself begging. With his fingers crossed, he implored through gritted teeth, "Come on, come on, get in the lift together, don't be shy. It's too hot to walk upstairs, get in the lift together, don't be shy, go on, for fuck's sake, GO ON."

When a third person suddenly appeared, well, Wilmo couldn't believe his eyes. An incredible twist of fate. A deserved stroke of luck, at last, after the disaster of *Agreed Statement*.

Seeing the three of them entering the elevator, Wilmo and Walter hugged each other, screaming for joy.

The idea was to keep the game going for a few hours, film everything, and edit the material so that they had enough for ten episodes. In the meantime, they hoped something interesting would happen in that elevator, something surprising. They needed rock-solid ratings for this show. The kind of ratings no one could argue with.

Whenever anyone who lived in the building tried to get in, Wilmo ran out of the Transit van and intercepted them at the main entrance. He introduced himself, said he was from a TV station, and asked the person not to use the elevator because – he said in an exaggeratedly serious tone, pointing to the control booth – they were shooting a reality show in the building. Then he gave these anonymous neighbours their fifteen minutes of fame by interviewing them. Did they know the girl with green hair? Or the young man with the piercing? Or the Elvis lookalike with the huge sideburns?

Those three people didn't know it yet, but they were about to become the stars of a new reality show with the provisional title *Blackout*.

The whole time, Wilmo played games with his unwitting protagonists. The altered doors, the lights turned off by remote control, the small, illusory movements of the elevator. It was just like when he was a child, and he shut the lizards up in the mayonnaise jar and then amused himself by putting the jar in the refrigerator, throwing it in the air, placing it on the lavatory, hoping that the lizards would go crazy with the noise and the vibrations.

Once they had shot sufficient material, Wilmo and Walter would free the trapped lizards and silence any possible hysterical reaction with a very substantial cheque offered by the network. Not to mention the chance to become well-known faces on TV.

But those carefully laid plans melted like an icicle in the sun, soon after midnight.

With the horrendous *splat!* of a man's skull being smashed between the steel doors.

When Ferro died between the doors, Walter went crazy. "Let's stop everything!" he started yelling. "Let's stop everything! Let's get them out! Let's get them out of there!"

But Wilmo, unable to take his eyes off the monitors, stopped him and told him to wait. He was watching something horrible, a man with his head between the doors, a boy wounded and bleeding.

But he was also seeing fantastic audience ratings.

Rock-solid ratings.

236

Success.

So he calmed Walter down.

And the game went on.

"We'll end up in prison," Walter says again, wringing his hands, his eyes watery. "I told you, let's end it here, I told you, let's get them out of there, it was an accident, it isn't our fault, how were we to know the man had a knife? We could have got away with it if we'd finished it there and then. We could have got away with it somehow, before."

Wilmo isn't listening to him, he never has. He's looking at the embers of his cigarette. Thinking of a way to emerge triumphant from this situation.

An extreme bluff. The last throw of the dice.

"Let's think this through," he says, in a grave voice, talking more to himself than to his theoretical partner. "Why did the man have a knife in his pocket? Why was he behaving like a homicidal maniac towards the end? Is it possible there's something we don't know about him, something potentially interesting?"

"I don't know, Wilmo, I don't know, I don't give a damn if he was a normal guy or if he liked buggering kittens, I don't care. We watched him die and we did nothing, we let the boy bleed for hours and we did nothing, oh, God, Wilmo, this time we won't get away with it, we won't get away with it, this time."

Wilmo stubs out his cigarette and stands up. He looks Walter in the eyes. "Of course we'll get away with it," he says. "Now listen to me. Listen carefully."

Walter runs his hands through his hair. He's shaking. "I'm listening."

237

"Good. Now, if we tell the truth. If we confess that we were here in the control booth, with our monitors, watching the idiot dying and the boy bleeding. That we saw all this, and still decided to leave them in there and carry on filming. If we confess all that, we're fucked. There's no way we'd get away with it. The death of the guy with the knife, yes, maybe, it all happened too quickly, there was no way we could have stopped it. But the boy, well, whichever way you look at it, we should have helped him and we didn't. We won't get away with it." He lowers his voice. "If we tell the whole truth, of course."

Walter is hanging on his every word, looking at him with eyes full of hope, like a drowning man. "Tell me you have a plan to get out of this mess, Wilmo. I beg you. Tell me. I beg you."

"Of course I have a plan." He puts a hand on his shoulder, almost paternally. "Listen carefully. This is what we'll say."

And he talks for a quarter of an hour, while the shadow of the tower block becomes ever more distinct around the Transit van.

Final Hour

Now, at last, it's all clear to her, all perfectly clear. Nothing happened, it was all a nightmare, a long, strange nightmare.

She goes over it all from the beginning. She runs it back in her mind, starting from one specific point.

She gets off the bus.

She searches for her keys.

A boy holds the main door open for her.

She thanks him with a slight smile.

They wait for the elevator.

A man with huge sideburns appears.

He mutters a perfunctory greeting.

The elevator arrives.

Claudia gets in first, followed by the boy, then by the man with the big sideburns.

The elevator ascends unhurriedly, the way it always does. They each get off at their own floor, the boy, the Elvis lookalike. They each go back to their own lives. Their paths will never cross again.

Claudia opens the door to her apartment. She takes off her uniform. She gets in the shower.

She lets the water run. She savours the touch of it on her skin. She opens her mouth. She drinks. She searches for the soap. She finds Ferro's crushed head.

She screams. She tries to step out of the shower, but outside the shower there's a wall of solid stone. The water has turned boiling hot. It burns like a dragon's breath.

"You have to take your armour off," Ferro's head suggests. "You have to take your armour off. You'll never get out if you don't take your armour off."

Claudia obeys.

(the ringing of a mobile phone, from another world)

Her skin has been eaten away by the scorching water, and she tears it off, inch by inch. When she's finished, she knows, she will be thin enough to slither out.

(it's going down)

When she's nothing but a skeleton, she smiles and slips out. She's greeted by thunderous applause, spotlights, hysterical screams.

(it's stopping)

Ferro is wearing Elvis's stage costume. He holds out the microphone to her. "You're looking really good, Claudia," he says. "What can you tell us about this experience?"

(voices on the other side of the door)

The audience is making too much noise. Ferro smiles and asks for a little silence.

"Well," Claudia answers, shaking hands with enthusiastic admirers, "What can I say? Never go into a tunnel in armour, and always take two or even three bottles of water with you."

"That's our Claudia," Ferro warbles. "Witty as ever." Good publicity. Claudia bows to the audience.

The Curtain Rises

The elevator door opens. Wilmo steps into the elevator. Startled, he gives a grimace of disgust.

Claudia is standing just inside the doors, bloodstained and smiling.

"I have to sign a release form, right?" she says in a shrill voice. "Do you know when this'll be going out? I want to tell my parents."

Her teeth are very white, blinding in the morning light.

Six Months Later

Claudia and Tomas are side by side in the middle of the studio, surrounded by the comedians, the sword swallower, the old-time singers, the man who trains worms, and the entire cast of the Italian soap *Waiting for a Sunny Day*, all bunched together under the spotlights.

The Sunday afternoon family show has stopped for a commercial break. Mr Fix-It is taking advantage of the break to touch up his make-up, while a singer in a toupee is using the opportunity to chat up a beautiful actress from the soap.

Claudia is still wearing the Lara Croft costume they made her wear just twenty minutes ago for a pathetic sketch with the comedians. Tomas is wearing a T-shirt with the *Blackout* logo, a *Blackout* baseball cap, a *Blackout* hooded sweatshirt. There are twenty or thirty teenagers in the audience dressed exactly like him, girls screaming and holding up placards with his name surrounded by little hearts. Backstage, Wilmo and Walter are biting the production manager's head off over something or other. They've become so important, they could bite the heads off God and all his archangels if they wanted to.

The media launch of *Blackout* was brilliant, everything they could have hoped for.

At the beginning of September, when the Italians re-
turned en masse from their holidays, the TV news reports
and the press were full of an incredible news item: on the
night of the August Bank Holiday, two poor young people
had been trapped in an elevator with a homicidal maniac.
By a strange coincidence, a camera had filmed the whole
thing. The footage, now in the process of being edited, was
said to be so remarkable that it was going to be shown as a
TV documentary – in episodes, because of the length.

The career of the homicidal maniac was revealed to the
public in great detail.

The videos found in the apartment on the twentieth floor
threw light on a whole series of mysterious disappearances,
and on the gruesome activities of Aldo Ferro and his
accomplice Gianfabio Brandauer, a well-known dentist
who had died some time earlier. The police investigation
led to a shack in the woods, a poor mad wretch tied to a
chair, and a freezer full of grisly remains. Naturally, viewers
were spared nothing.

Ferro's father-in-law reacted by putting on his full-dress
uniform and hanging himself, unable to bear the shame.
The maniac's wife vanished with her son, to escape being
hounded by the press.

Thanks to this shrewd media campaign, and to the
few, contradictory pieces of information allowed to filter
through, there was a feeling of growing anticipation before
the first episode of *Blackout*. Wilmo and Walter revealed
nothing about what was to be broadcast, but they were
quite lavish with details of how that rough-and-ready but
extraordinary footage had come to be shot.

It had all started out as an idea for a harmless reality show about how Italians behave in elevators, they said, how people pretend to search for their keys, or talk about the weather between floors; in other words, a fairly mild piece of pop sociology. The plan had been to start filming in September, but the cameras had been put in early, over August Bank Holiday, taking advantage of the holiday period in order to work in peace.

Then, when the cameras were already in place, the blackout happened.

A trick of fate.

It was pure *chance* that the elevator had broken down with three people inside. And it was *chance* too that the cameras, which had their own independent electricity supply, had been automatically activated by the short circuit and had filmed everything that had taken place in the elevator.

Arriving in the morning, Wilmo and Walter had been puzzled to discover how much energy had been consumed. Running to the elevator to check, they had discovered what had happened and freed Claudia and Tomas. As an explanation, this was all somewhat wanting, but then the images did show Wilmo entering the elevator and rescuing Claudia and Tomas, didn't they?

To be honest, there were so many holes in this version of events, you could have driven a truck through it. But weren't the Italians the people who had made the bosses of private television millionaires? Hadn't the Italians swallowed fifty years of the most complete bullshit, dubious official explanations for how an aeroplane just happened to blow up in mid-air off the coast of Italy, or how an anti-globalization demonstrator just happened to be hit by a stray bullet, things like that?

If they had swallowed all that, while remaining convinced that they were clever, really clever, the cleverest people in the world, well, couldn't they also swallow a story about TV cameras with minds of their own? And besides, there had been a report by technical experts, which had confirmed Wilmo and Walter's version of events.

Obviously, the report had been a complete fake. The result, as usual, of a couple of phone calls by Mr Fix-It.

But the Italian people didn't know any of this.

They had swallowed it all, and even enjoyed the taste.

So, with the ground prepared and expectation well stoked, the whole of Italy sat down to watch the first episode of *Blackout*. At last.

The next day, in offices, on buses, in schools, it was all anyone was talking about.

Tomas, the sweet sixteen-year-old adored by mothers, grandmothers and young girls!

Claudia, apparently frail, but hard as nails and as tough as a ninja!

Ferro, outwardly respectable if eccentric, but in reality a nasty homicidal maniac!

What would happen to those two poor young people trapped in an elevator? How long would Aldo Ferro be able to control his predatory instincts?

The whole country was infected by *Blackout* fever. It was like a kind of collective insanity at every level of society.

The comments of a few isolated sceptics – about the strange way the doors had worked, for example, or the curious coincidence that all three mobile phones were out of use at the same time – were dismissed as the paranoid ravings of conspiracy theorists, or the sniping of snobbish intellectuals who considered themselves superior to the masses.

The cliffhanger at the end of the fifth episode – Aldo Ferro stabbing Tomas and then turning threateningly to Claudia, one second before the end credits! – chilled an entire nation.

When Wilmo and Walter were handed the ratings for the sixth episode, the episode where Aldo Ferro died, they were speechless. They just looked at each other, shaking with emotion, their eyes watering.

Mr Fix-It appeared in person to congratulate his son and his son's brilliant partner. Bringing with him, as a theatrical gesture, a bottle of Cristal and three glasses.

That was when Wilmo and Walter realized they'd made it.

While the programme was hypnotizing the nation, Tomas and Claudia were being looked after in a private clinic, at the network's expense. Isolated, anonymous and protected: until the last episode of *Blackout,* nobody was to know what finally happened to the two young people in the elevator. The only exceptions were Francesca and Bea, who were allowed to visit the clinic only after signing all kinds of confidentiality forms.

Francesca appeared at the clinic with a broken arm and a black eye.

A fall on the stairs.

Or so she said.

The network had hired a whole team of lawyers ready to defend Claudia against accusations of murder, in case anyone cast doubt on the self-defence hypothesis. It had also destroyed the tapes of the interviews with the neighbours, and silenced those same neighbours with some fairly substantial cheques.

Immediately after the final triumphant episode of *Blackout*, the isolation came to an end. On the Sunday afternoon family show, the heroes from the elevator were at last displayed to the world.

Tomas and Claudia appeared to a truly delirious welcome. People going crazy, yelling, girls with huge placards, flashlights popping, bombastic music, their names being screamed over and over. They looked at each other, confused and scared.

The network also arranged a fake reunion, broadcast live: Tomas and Francesca pretended to meet again for the first time since Tomas had been trapped in the elevator. The whole thing was stage-managed down to the last detail, but mothers and grandmothers wept buckets over it. Cleverly assuming his most fatherly tone, Mr Fix-It placed his hands on Tomas and Francesca's shoulders and said, "Children, I know that before that terrible thing happened in the elevator you were planning to get married, but listen to me, don't be in any hurry, you're young, finish school first and then decide what you want to do, all right?"

The whole audience was on its feet, applauding.

The network didn't plan a similar encounter for Claudia. Her relationship with Bea wasn't exactly in tune with the family orientation of the Sunday afternoon show.

The network bosses did suggest to Claudia that she should appear with a pretend boyfriend, maybe a bit alternative, a bit anti-globalization, but then they changed their minds and decided to present her as the Bad Girl, the tough cookie who terrifies men. Claudia didn't mind that idea. At least she would avoid the nonsense of the pretend boyfriend.

The meeting with Bea in the clinic had been brief and embarrassing. Claudia couldn't think of anything to say to her, anything at all. The elevator had chewed her up and spat her out, reshaping her in the process, and the new Claudia didn't feel she had anything in common any more with the people she'd cared about in her previous life.

It was something she talked about at length with her new therapist, at the Tuesday sessions paid for by the network.

The commercial break is nearly over. They've just shown a preview of the reborn Giampi Supermaxihero, exhumed at Tomas's express request.

At the beginning, the heroes of *Blackout* could have asked for anything. If Tomas had asked to become a member of U2, well, Mr Fix-It would have made Bono and The Edge a persuasive little speech convincing them to relaunch as a five-piece group with an extra guitarist.

Tomas had exploited this absolute power to make his Francesca happy. The Supermaxihero had cried with joy over that pathetic act of charity, embracing Tomas with tears in his eyes and repeating, "My boy, my boy," unable to let go of him.

Claudia and Tomas were the centrepiece of the show for four or five weeks, but in the end, well, there are only so many times you can explain how Aldo Ferro was brought down with a judo move, or how to break a serial killer's eardrum with a basement key. Gradually, interest in the two of them levelled off, and over the next few Sundays the crude Roman comedian, the chorus girls and the gossip columnists regained the territory they had lost.

Claudia and Tomas were reduced to being a mere presence, while the network tried to find other outlets for them. For Claudia they already had a role lined up as a sexy spy in a blatant rip-off of *Nikita*. For Tomas, they were thinking of a music show aimed fair-and-square at a youth audience.

In the meantime here they still were, mixed in with the sword swallower, the man who trained worms, the comedians, the cast of the soap opera.

"Is that your girlfriend in the front row?" Claudia whispers.

"Yes," Tomas replies. "Francesca."

Claudia smiles derisively in a way that curiously recalls the way Aldo Ferro sneered at them. "Does your girlfriend know about the cut scene?"

Tomas looks at her, puzzled. "What cut scene?"

"Ah," she says softly. "You're out of touch. There's a rumour doing the rounds on the internet that the producers of *Blackout* cut a sex scene. Somewhere around the twelfth hour."

He winces. "What sex scene?" he asks, making sure he's not heard by the man who trains worms.

"The sex scene between the two of us," she says with that same sneering smile. "I'm supposed to have practically raped you. They say the producers cut it because you're a minor, but now the cut scene is one of the most persistent urban myths on the net."

Tomas turns red. "No, it isn't true," he stammers. "It never happened."

"You'd have liked to, though," Claudia says.

Fortunately, just then the commercials come to an end. Mr Fix-It has finished having his make-up touched up, and now he's calling the troops to order.

Tomas doesn't like talking to Claudia very much any more. It's quite unsettling, talking to Claudia.

The same Claudia who stares into space and moves mechanically, with a remote, inscrutable little smile.

The band starts to play a medley of old hits. The whole cast sing along roughly to a hotchpotch of tunes in which *La Bamba* segues without a break into *Voglio andare a vivere in campagna* and then into *Azzurro*.

Claudia and Tomas are in the middle of this absurd vortex, sucked in by the lights, the wildly clapping audience, the urgent rhythms of the band, and because it's on TV everything moves quickly, so quickly that you can't get out of the vortex, you really can't.

So when the band launches into *Brazil*, Tomas places his hands on Claudia's shoulders, and Claudia places hers on the shoulders of the sword swallower in front of her.

And, swaying their hips in time to the music, they join the conga line.